MERCILESS PUNKS

DOLLS AND DOUCHEBAGS PART THREE

MADELINE FAY

Dedicated to big dick energy and coffee.
The most important things that get us through the day.

TRIGGER WARNING

This is a dark, bully theme, and enemies-to-lovers romance story ending with a cliffhanger. A why choose romance where the heroine won't have to choose between her different love interests.

This book contains graphic and violent scenes, including rape, physical and emotional violence, child abuse, swearing, sexual scenes, PTSD, and MM. Suitable only for readers aged 18+.

Chapter Ten contains light MM

Spoiler: This series does NOT contain cheating.

Please do not take this warning lightly if you are sensitive to any of the triggers listed above.

This is Part Three of Dolls and Douchebags, which does end with a HEA eventually.

If you have any issues regarding the book, please reach out to the author using one of the links on the last page.

PROLOGUE

Rig

"I need you to do this one last favor for me before it's too late." I lean against the hood of my car, tossing the wrench onto the workbench when silence meets me on the other end of the phone. "Pike, I'm running out of time."

I'm fucking desperate and I know he can hear it in my tone, I'm practically begging here.

"We shouldn't even be talking over the phone. It's too dangerous. If he finds out..." Pike trails off, his voice raspy because he knows that if Payne finds out... we're both dead.

"This will be my last favor, brother. He's watching her too closely. I thought I had time but she's growing into a woman now. You know what that means. Especially since she doesn't look like him. Everyone can see it, man. I've run out of options." I run my hand through my long hair, noticing the grey strands that weren't there a few years ago.

Time is flying by. I'm not as young as I used to be, nor am I strong enough to take care of my most important treasure.

"When?" That's all Pike says as he draws out a long breath.

"I'd say right fucking now but too many eyes on her at the moment. That fucking kid keeps following her around even when she doesn't notice. I don't like it, the way he stares at her. Fucking hell, I've even told him to stay away from her but he just looks at me with these dead, blue eyes." I push off the hood of the car and start to pace while looking left and right to make sure the garage is empty.

"I'll see what I can do. This is my last favor, my friend. I have my own club to worry about, I can't start a war with Payne. Hell's Devils doesn't compare in numbers. Plus my boy is the only thing left I have and I'm not willing to lose him no matter what." Pike gets straight to the point, telling me that he'll cut all connections for the sake of his son.

"I understand. Just find me a way for her to disappear, a place where he can't find her. She'll be sixteen soon and I don't want this life for her. She's already seen the hardships and the way the world works by being here at the compound. I want something better for her where she'll never have to fear or look over her shoulder." I pause at the sound of the garage door opening, heading over to the bay doors and finding no one there but the empty parking lot.

"Give me a week." Pike lets out a heavy sigh over the phone. I can picture him opening his desk drawer and pulling out a bottle of whiskey.

Being the president of a motorcycle club ages you fast, it's one thing after another but I'm glad he has my back. I'll always owe him for what he did sixteen years ago but I might just owe him my life now. I hear a bang and whip my head towards the sound only to find that kid staring at me from across the lot by the fire barrels.

"A Demon Jokers owes you one. I have to go." I end the call without looking away from him, his face cast in shadows from the dancing flames of the fire as he lights a cigarette.

He inhales and holds it in for a second too long before blowing the smoke towards my direction. Blue eyes hold mine without blinking and I swear I see a crack of a smile before he tosses the bud of his cigarette into the fire and walks back into the building without looking back.

I lean my shoulder against the garage door opening as the psychopath kid walks away, I rub my hand over my chest, the pressure tight.

Fucking Cruz.

Gazing around, I make sure my precious treasure isn't hanging around with Cruz and sigh with relief when I don't see her outside. Feeling my heart racing, I grab the chain-link above my head and close up the garage bay door before heading inside. I have to keep an eye on her at all times; something keeps telling me that she's going to get hurt and I won't be here to save her.

Impending doom.

CHAPTER 1

Tillie

Why does the sound of a zipper being lowered hit me like a gunshot going off and make my whole body shake like the end of a rattlesnake's tail? I hate how the mind can be triggered by just a smell, a word, or a sound. Fuck if the noise of Payne's pants zipper slowly lowering doesn't make my mouth burn with bile. What's happening to me this very minute, seconds from being violated again, has my limbs frozen in stark fear. Everything he just said is whipping through my brain, trying to cut me open to get into my mind and leave me stuck with only my own voice to keep me company.

"Wh–what do you mean? I don't... No! You're lying..." I trail off on a broken whisper, my body going completely flush until it feels like someone dropped a bucket of ice-cold water over me and leaving the meat suit I'm wearing numb.

It's like I've been placed in a body that isn't mine and I'm left with not knowing who I am. I should be jumping for joy, thanking a faceless God that Payne isn't my father. Instead, I feel cheated. Why have me go through the same torment all those years, making me feel like I've only been a piece of trash placed in front of him when in reality I could have had a father that would cherish me? It's funny how life works that way but I'm still not laughing. Maybe the loud, crazed laughter echoing around the kitchen is mine but who knows? It could all just be in my head because I truly think I'm crashing at a rapid speed, watching everything in slow motion just before I realize it's all happening within a blink of an eye. I'm almost at the point of not caring what the outcome is anymore.

"You think my daughter would be a slut like you? You're just like your mother, willing to open her legs for anyone, and now I'll be ripping through your tight pussy to get a taste of what's mine. I fed you, clothed you, put a roof over your goddamn head. It's only fair I sink my dick into what I rightfully own," Payne taunts while sliding a knife through the back strap of my bra and leaving me naked except for the thin pair of underwear that I wish was glued to my body.

"Is that why you let your men rape me? Make me feel like I was nothing? Nothing. Nothing. Nothing." I keep repeating that one stupid word like a scratched record as the back of my neck is held down by the palm of Payne's hand.

I guess I have my answer as to why I've always called him by his first name instead of Dad. He never felt like one and didn't deserve the title. My gaze connects with Dalton's and I realize I've been staring at him this whole time while losing my mind. Maybe this is just a horrible nightmare, where all my truths come out to play while the guy with the violet eyes watches my past repeat itself right in front of him as he slowly bleeds to death.

Please don't die. Don't die in front of me like this.

"Tillie." Payne grabs my neck and roughly brings me to a standing position with my back arched as my bra slides down my arms, exposing my breasts to Whiskey and Poe and their disgusting, lust-filled eyes. "You are nothing. I just had to remind you and set an example. You can thank your whore of a mother for that." His voice is like slick oil on my skin that I desperately want to wash off.

If I could, I'd vomit all over the quartz counters but I can't even draw in a proper breath to try. Lead sits heavy in my stomach and the sharp, stinging pain that trails down my collarbone to my hip bone tells me I'm wide awake. Maybe if I focus on something to block out everything, I can live through this again. Why would I want to though? What more is there for me? I remember that stupid fucking nail in the basement ceiling and how it gave me the sanity to escape but that part of my mind I hold onto is going to crack this time around.

My body was used like a rag doll, being tossed and turned on numb limbs as if my body wasn't my own. I really did die that day. The only thing that my eyes connect with are Dalton's and it's the sheer madness, uncontrolled rage shining in his gaze that grounds me.

It says fight.

Live.

You would think that another cut on my body, another scar, wouldn't hurt me since I'm used to it but it still brings tears to my eyes. I won't give Payne my voice though, it's the one thing I have left. Knowing he's digging his dirty nails down my skin, drawing blood, fills me with disgust. It's like he's trying to mark me until he's embedded in my soul so I'll always feel dirty and be reminded of him.

"Dalton," I choke out quietly, feeling my unblinking eyes fill with more tears as Payne cups the front of my underwear, groping me tightly through the thin material.

Just when he starts to slide my panties to the side, Poe rubbing his hands together like he's in for a fine meal, and Whiskey groaning as he palms his hard-on, the sound of the garage door creaking on its hinges makes everyone freeze.

"Whiskey, door. Poe, on the other side." Payne barks out

orders in a rough voice but doesn't move from behind me as he snaps the elastic of my panties back in place.

He doesn't seem to have any fear, thinking he can get away with anything as if he's God himself. I can't wait for the day he realizes he can bleed too, so I can watch the light fade from his eyes. I'm counting down those days when I'm strong enough to be the one delivering his death.

I don't dare to move an inch as the garage door to the mudroom opens and shuts. The sound of Diana's high laugh and the clicking of her heels makes my eyes connect with Dalton's again. Seeing his gaze already burning into mine helps remind me I'm not completely alone this time. Though I'd rather he not see what's coming, I have to swallow the shame because no one really wants someone to know their deepest, darkest secrets. To have them exposed. I wanted to tell my life story in my own time but I guess plans don't always go how we want them to. Dalton keeps slowly shaking his head from side to side, blinking rapidly as his chin keeps dropping to his chest. He's going to pass out soon and maybe that's a good thing, he won't have to see my body being raped. He keeps grinding his teeth around the gag in his mouth, baring his white teeth and straining his body around the ropes as if trying to find the strength to break free. I know he's in pain on the outside and inside by the haunted shadow in his violet eyes. If I could, I'd stab Payne in the exact same spot he stabbed Dalton, over and over and over again. Dalton is in pain because of me. This is all my fault. Had it not been for me, Dalton's dad wouldn't be dead. The guy I'm starting to really care about wouldn't be bleeding out in front of me while strapped to a chair. Logan wouldn't be knocked out upstairs. I've done nothing but bring them pain. I'm a disturbance they never needed.

All of it is my fucking fault.

Diana's laughter cuts off to a sudden halt, her voice caught on a gasp as she stares at Payne like she's seen a ghost.

"You dare enter my house! Do you know who the fuck I am? Fucking Demon Jokers scum!" Franco's sudden angry, booming shout makes me jump and I turn my head to see him standing, frozen in place by the fridge with a gun pointed to the side of his head.

"Like we give a fuck who you are. I'm the guy holding a gun to your fucking head, seconds away from splattering your brain all over the place." Whiskey smirks, his yellow teeth flashing, making me cringe as he digs the gun harder against Franco's temple.

"Well, well. It's been a long time hasn't it, Diana? So this is where you've been hiding? In a life of expensive shit and a big house over your head. I thought you would be rotting in a gutter somewhere but I should have known you'd spread those legs for anything or anyone with money," Payne sneers, his rotting breath filling my lungs as he leans over my shoulder to rest his chin there as he taunts Diana.

"Y–you can't be here. It's not possible. I've hidden and covered all my tracks," Diana whispers in agony before flashing her eyes to me, taking in my naked state with a grimace and disgust outlined on her face.

"You're all dead men. I'm going to put a bullet in each of you," Franco states calmly, but his clenched jaw gives away how pissed he really is.

You don't take away control from a man like Franco who's had a taste of power, he'll do anything to keep it from being stolen from him. Anything.

"It's almost laughable how you think I'm here for you, Diana, but the timing couldn't be more perfect. You'll get to watch while I have my way with your daughter, but I think I'll let the man of the house have the first taste. What do you say, Franco? You want a taste of this sweet pussy?" Payne makes sure to face me fully towards Franco, causing me to flinch as his eyes can't help but roam up and down my body before his expression hardens.

"No!" Diana shouts as Poe grabs her from behind and locks his arms around her with a laugh as she starts bucking wildly in his grip and something in my chest tightens as I think she's trying to fight to save me but once again I'm fooled. "Let him go, Payne, Franco has nothing to do with this. He and I will walk out of here and not say anything," she pleads desperately.

I look away from her gaze when it collides with mine, seeing her lips twisting with rage. Can't say I blame her. I brought the devil to her doorstep when all I wanted was to find someplace safe to call my own. Poe tightens his grip on her and shoves her arms behind her back while roughly grabbing her chin so she can't look away from me.

"Can't pass up some sweet pussy and let me tell you... she's tight as fuck." Whiskey laughs as he cocks the gun and places it at the back of Franco's head to make him move around the kitchen island until he's a few feet away from me.

"Remember this moment, Tillie. Your actions caused deaths like Doris and a trail of blood of Hell's Devils to find you here. You'll take whatever I throw at you. Now be a good girl and spread your legs apart so your stepfather can shove his tongue inside your cunt. Maybe if you're really good, I'll tell you who your real dad is," Payne whispers in my ear, making me feel like cement is holding my feet down as I drown in my mind. I can somewhat hear over the buzzing in my ears as Dalton screams behind his gag, but all I can focus on is Franco being kicked behind his knees to fall in front of me.

I see his cold eyes staring at Payne for a split second, promising death but what has me sucking in a ragged breath is the desire he's trying to hide behind a blank expression as he finally gazes up into my eyes.

A loud thump above our heads makes Franco's lips curl at the edges in the beginning of a grin before it's gone. It takes me a second to realize that not once has he asked about Logan's whereabouts.

"Whiskey, I thought you said you took care of his son? Go get him and bring him down here so he can watch his father enjoy his girl's pussy," Payne orders with a harsh laugh as Whiskey tosses the gun carelessly to him and winks at me before striding out of the kitchen and into the dark part of the house.

"Now, where were we? Oh yes. Chief." Payne makes sure to point the gun under the left side of my jawline so I can still watch Franco even as he digs the cold metal into my skin. "Take her panties off."

I must be going crazy because with the gun no longer pointing at Franco, he doesn't try to fight or do anything really but keeps his gaze directed between my legs. Why do his hands lift and grasp my hips before slowly sliding down to clasp the edge of my lace underwear? Some crazy part of me thinks he's enjoying this.

"Will you look at that? Doesn't matter if you're covered in paint and dirty, it seems your step daddy dearest wants some young pussy." I can feel the sleazy grin that crosses Payne's face as he lays his cheek against mine to watch Franco over my shoulder.

"You son of bitch! I left and never looked back! You can't do this!" Diana sobs and I can't look towards her but it doesn't matter, not like I want to. As expected, I can feel the accusatory glare she's directing at me and it's slowly eating my flesh away like maggots.

I do feel dirty and gross. It's nothing like when my four assholes touch me. Even if that gangster, Dom, touched me, I wouldn't feel revolted by his touch like I do right now by Franco. All of this is wrong. So wrong on so many levels and there's nothing I can do about it. My gaze tries to connect with Dalton so I don't have to witness another tearing pain in my soul that will keep me up at night but Payne has other plans.

The pressure of the gun leaves my jaw and I see his arm raise to my right, pointing at Dalton who, thank God, by some miracle has passed out. He doesn't need to see my shame, to fill the blank spaces in his head.

"None of that, Tillie. You're going to watch the most powerful man in L.A. destroy you. That innocence you try to hold onto died a long time ago when I had my men rip your pussy in two. Tonight... it's time you lost all hope. This is your life now. Give up and give in to me."

Why do those words make me feel like the earth is pressing on my shoulders and my heart is sinking at the same time? Give up... Give in... Just let it all go and accept that this is all I'll ever know. For the first time ever, tears leak down my cheeks as Payne gains another piece of my soul in his dirty palm that has shaken hands with the devil.

"I hate you," I whisper those words out loud. To whom? I'm not sure.

It could be Payne for all he's put me through or it could be Franco as I watch him slide my underwear the rest of the way off as if in a daze. This is really happening yet I feel frozen, as if my body is shutting down and quitting. Maybe it's both men who can't keep their fucking hands to themselves. I never asked for this.

"What are you waiting for, Chief? What does she taste like?" Payne asks, taunting him.

I want to squeeze my eyes shut, but for some reason, I can't. It's like I want to torture myself, beating myself up just to feel that ounce of pain I deserve. There must be a reason this keeps happening to me? Either way, I watch Franco lean in, as if mesmerized and take a deep breath with his face inches from my pussy. The huff of his warm breath causes me to jump in place, his gaze flickering up to watch me as he licks with the flat of his tongue between my legs. His tongue is wet, warm, and moves rapidly, going right in for the kill without intent of slowing down.

More tears flow down my cheeks, hating myself for liking how good it feels, even as much as I hate every second of this. I try to fight it by putting my mind somewhere else, but my body is reacting no matter how much I don't want this. The wetness between my thighs mortifies me. He sucks my clit between his lips suddenly and sucks hard enough to bruise as he watches my hips jerk forward as he grabs the back of my thighs to bring me closer to his mouth. I'm surrounded by two monsters that get off on my suffering and humiliation.

"You may say no but it seems your body tells a different story. Once a whore, always a whore." Payne laughs evilly in my ear as my body shakes, an uncontrolled orgasm rising to the surface.

"I–I don't want this," I manage to say in a shaky voice, squeezing my eyes shut for a second as I try to hold off as long as I can.

"Lies. I better see his face covered in your juices, Tillie, or I'm blowing off your boyfriend's head over here." He wiggles his gun in Dalton's direction as if I need a reminder of what's at stake.

My body slumps in Payne's hold in defeat. I'll never have control of my body or my mind it seems. Why fight? I don't want Dalton to die. I'll do anything for my guys to make sure they survive, to experience a long life of actually living. This right here isn't living, it's trying to survive even when you can hear the clock ticking. Any moment, my life can end and I can only recall a few times I've truly felt happy. I fight with myself back and forth, trying to find the will to keep going but it's like grasping at air...

This is me giving up.

Forgive me. I think about the guys and hope they come to realize this isn't the real me. My brain and body are at war with each other. My traitorous body is winning.

"You have one second to let go of my girl or fucking die."

CHAPTER 2

Tey

"*Y*ou put my precious in danger and caused my unicorn harm! I'm going to cut you open. I'm going to enjoy ripping your intestines out and shoving them down your throat until they spill out of your stomach all over again. But I won't, at least not before you tell us why you were at the rave. After that? Well..." I smirk and shrug my shoulders before holding my knife up to the single light bulb hanging in the middle of the room and squint my eyes... Is that a scuff mark on my knife?

Fucking great. Another thing tonight that puts me in a bad mood. First, Tillie almost gets hurt in a shootout of guns, my stuffed unicorn's head pops off, and now a scratch on my favorite knife. Where did I go wrong in my life to deserve this? All I want is to stab this fucker like five minutes ago, give my knife a nice polish to make her shine again, and bury my face in Tillie's neck or pussy. I'm not picky as long as I get to draw in her sweet cinnamon and vanilla scent.

"Tey, focus," Nicky orders as he circles around the gang member tied to the chair like a shark drawing closer to its prey, the deep timbre of his voice causing a shiver to trail down my spine in delight at the quiet demand.

When he's ready, I'll be bottom. Of course I won't tell him that just yet. He's got to work for it. If he wants to shove his big, tattoo-covered cock up my tight ass he's going to have to open up for all the love I have for him. Jin pushed him and beat him since I've known Nicky, and if his father ever finds out that his heir, his son, likes the taste of men too... his body would be found behind some restaurant dumpster in downtown Chinatown with everyone turning a blind eye. I don't think my Nicholas will resist the temptation of me much longer. I'll keep him safe no matter what, and I mean, come on, have you seen my glutes? Fucking squeezable, I've worked my ass off to get these muscles on my butt.

How can I focus at a time like this when all that's been playing in my mind for the last two nights is him and Tillie sharing my cum in a kiss that made me hard in one second flat all over again. He's not helping matters when he steps around me, his long fingers skimming the back of my neck as he moves to crouch in front of our latest torture victim. I've been dreaming for a couple years now of those skilled fingers wrapping around my thick cock, coating his hands with squirt after squirt of my delicious cum.

Maybe next time I'll carve my name into his chest, and watch as his pale skin turns red with his warm blood. Anyone who would look at him would know he belongs to me. Oh! Maybe we should get matching tattoos? I'll let him tattoo my cock if I get to pierce his and if I'm lucky, Tillie will let me tattoo her pussy? A nipple piercing on her would be fucking delicious too. Ugh! There's so much to consider! I would love to see my name on her body, placed over one of her scars that will now bring her only memories of me instead. She might not let me mark her body with tattoos or piercings but then again I'll just have to knock her out with one of Nicky's drugs if it comes to that. She'll just wake up all dazed and bam. New artwork that I created forever on her skin! God, she could wake up with the needle piercing her pink nipples and cursing me in Spanish once she realizes what I did. Just the thought alone has me ready to come, my balls aching. I bite my knuckle to quiet my groan and Nicky glances over his shoulder with his eyebrow raised before his eyes slide down to the obvious tent in my pants with a smirk.

"This can go two different ways. You talk and I can make your death quick with just a shot to the back of the head, or I can drag it. Pain is like breathing and hours after I've had my fun by peeling layers of your skin off, all you'll know before your lungs expand one more time is pain," Nicky threatens the gang member, his green gaze unyielding and he slowly shakes his head at the stupidity when our guest remains quiet.

"So be it, buddy. Silence it is. It really doesn't take a genius to figure out which gang you belong to. You should have covered up those tattoos, Amigo." Nicky sighs like he has better things to be doing but I know he loves torturing those who deserve it just as much as I do.

I walk over to the chain-link fence in the corner of the room that has all of our favorite tools on hooks just for this occasion. I play with my lip ring, sucking it in and out as I debate which device I want to start with. Why is this so hard? The pliers or tire iron?

"Nicholas, help! Broken bones first or slow torture?" I glance over my shoulder to see his forearms rippling with muscles as he stands over our struggling guest.

Nicky grabs the jaw that's been clamped shut under our questioning while placing his other hand over the tattoo of a skull on the gang member's forehead to hold him still as Nicky pries his mouth open.

"Fuck you! I'm not saying shit!" He screams through the

pain and tries to wrench his head away but Nicky has a tight grip on him.

"Since you made your choice, I'm not seeing why you need your tongue," Nicky replies back casually like he's talking about a grocery shopping list and not about removing the fleshy meat in this asshole's mouth.

I'm starting to think maybe after he's done with his tongue, I should put it in a glass jar and give it to Tillie as a gift? Actions speak louder than words! I like this idea. With that in mind, I grab the pliers off the fence and practically skip over to Nicky's right side like a schoolgirl, but only because this is the exciting part of having a torture session.

"Any last words?" I laugh in the gang member's face as he glares up at me with a hint of fear in his eyes just as I grasp his wiggling tongue between the pliers and bend down to grab my knife out of my boot.

"Wa–wait! Jesus Christ! J-just wait, I'll tell you every-thing!" His words are hard to understand, likely due to all the saliva coming out of his mouth from his incessant babbling.

Gross.

I release the tool from his mouth just as the sound of Nicky's phone blares from his back pocket. I give him a nod that I got this as he steps away to answer with his shoulders dropping in disappointment. Like I said, that stone-cold expression doesn't fool me. He loves the sounds of screams when the flesh parts under his scalpel blade. With my back towards him and my focus on the fucker in front of me, I block out every other noise and pocket the pliers for now.

"Talk. Was this an attack on Franco or Dom?" I spin my knife between my fingers, already getting bored as he gasps for breath and tries to wipe the drool off his chin onto his shirt.

"You'll let me go if I talk, man? I'll flee the state and you won't ever see me again. I'm as good as dead if Hector catches me…" His voice trails off as I give him a blank look, not giving a shit that his boss is going to kill him.

"Yeah, pal, I'll let you go," I lie through my teeth, playing along, and hold up my finger in a pinky promise but drop it quickly when I remember his hands are tied behind his back.

I'm really not good at lying. *How embarrassing*, I think to myself with a low whistle through my teeth.

"Hector wants the girl." I watch his lips move, form words, but my whole body goes still and it's like the only thing I can see is blood before it even spills.

If he's talking about our Tillie, I'll kill every fucker who thinks they can take her away from me. The thought alone makes me see red. Red as I slit their throats, color my painting in gang members' blood, and more red as I display my artwork in Tillie's bedroom right over where she sleeps. She'll have only peaceful dreams at night knowing I'm cleaning the streets up so that she's protected.

I think I like this plan.

"What girl?" I ask very slowly, deadly, as I stop my knife mid spin.

"The slut who was dancing all over Dom. Demon Jokers want their property back. Cunt thought she could run away but when your daddy is the president of a fucking motorcycle club, word spreads fast. A pretty penny for her return. I heard the prez is already in Los Angeles." He shrugs his shoulders and looks up at me with hopeful eyes.

"His daughter?" I whisper the words and my expression must be scary as shit because he shrinks back in his seat and glances nervously around.

"You gonna let me go now? That's all I know. I swear." He nods his head in fast movements and wiggles in his seat before clearing his throat.

"I believe you. You've been most helpful," I say as I grab his head in a headlock and tip him back so he's looking up at me.

I eat up the fear in his eyes, especially as I raise my knife and hold it over his forehead, right above his ridiculous tattoo.

"The fuck, man! You said you would let me go!" he grunts out, his face turning a bright red as he struggles in my grip but it's useless.

"I lied. Now hold still. I'm just going to cut off your tattoo and have it delivered to Hector as a gift. Oh, and my lady is going to love having your tongue on her shelf. Souvenirs, am I right, man? The best gifts for someone special." I feel my body relax as the blade skims along the corner of his skull tattoo and blood begins to trail down his face.

I get in the zone, ignoring his ear-shattering screams, and slide my blade through his skin, the cut smooth like butter. The moment the missing piece of flesh off his forehead falls to the ground, I step back to admire my work. He does look better this way. If he was going to live after I'm done with him, I'd bet all the ladies would be falling all over him. My artist work is known around these parts. He would be fucking popular on display, even being dead and all.

Out of the corner of my eye, I see the glint of metal and hear the resounding boom before I feel the gang member's blood coating my face from the bullet wound between his eyes. I blink a couple of times and slowly face Nicky with my mouth hanging open like a gaping fish. Why does Nicky have to ruin my fun? I wasn't nearly done and I was just starting to have fun.

"What the hell?" I cross my arms, tapping my knife against my bicep as I glare at Nicky.

"We need to go now. Tillie called on Logan's phone sounding frantic and saying what sounded like a goodbye.

We need to get to his house. Now." His muscles are tight, ripping under his suit jacket and he turns without looking back at me, striding fast to the door in an almost robotic way.

I don't ask any more questions, not even glancing back at our guest with regret. I'll come back for the tongue later. My angel is in trouble. I just know it by how stiff Nicky is. By the time I'm busting out the door, his headlights are shining brightly at me as the engine purrs to life. He even reaches across the console to open my door before I can reach the car. Fuck. I hop in like my life depends on it and slam the door as he shifts gears, peeling out of the warehouse parking lot. The tires squeal from the burning rubber at the neck-breaking speed he takes off at.

I smell death on the horizon, bodies are going to drop tonight if someone harms one single hair on her head. Why did she call from Logan's phone? Did something happen to my brother from another mother? I urge Nicky to drive faster, picturing all the worst possible ways they could be in danger and my chest tightens at the thought of finding them dead. I'll protect my family at all cost, even if I'm up until dawn burying bodies to hide the evidence. The guys haven't admitted to having feelings for our girl, but I think it was love at first sight for me... pretty sure those dark eyes sucked my soul out and I just had to have her no matter what. I don't care what lengths I have to go to keep her by my side even if it requires her being handcuffed to my side for a very, long fucking time.

Our worlds collided like a car crash with shattered glass, our bodies airborne until we reached each other with open arms to embrace, the perfect fit, and now she's ours. I don't care who the fuck her dad is, he could be Jesus himself and I'd still corrupt her soul until she comes to terms that I'm never letting her go.

I ask myself how the hell I get into these messes, like how I'm scaling the side of Logan's house like a freaking ninja under the cloak of darkness and not falling to my death? Gripping the stone wall on the side of his home that leads to Tillie's balcony, tiny grains of stone bite into the palms of my hands but I grind my teeth as every muscle strains and I take the final leap over the ledge, out of breath like a chain-smoker.

"Fuckkkk. I need to lay off the junk food." I pat my abs while laying on the stone slab of her balcony, amazed at how defined my stomach still is after I've been stuffing my face with Twinkies along with flaming hot Cheetos.

Smoking weed makes you eat the craziest shit. I swear, I was craving pickles and ice cream like a pregnant woman just the other night. It's easier to lay off the drugs when Tillie is around but the moment she's out of my sight, it's like the itch under my skin burns until I'm digging my nails down my arms. I need to get the edge off and weed seems to make my mind go quiet, at least for a little while. Out of all the drugs, Tillie is the best. She's a dose that goes straight to my system and leaves me feeling like I'm floating.

Bouncing to my feet after catching my breath, I duck beneath her windows and sneak along the side of the house with my calf muscles burning from the climb. I look into her room through the windows only to see the bedroom coated in darkness. The French door's handles twist with ease under my hand, only a small squeak grinds on the hinges of the door as I slip through the open gap. I can hear my own breathing, loud to my own ears as I pad on silent feet across her carpet. The sound intensifies when I notice a dark spot on the floor at my feet that trails towards her closest.

I'd recognize that copper smell anywhere. Blood.

My heart pounds in hard, rapid beats. For the first time in my life, fear lives and breathes inside of me. What if... What if it's Tillie behind that closed door? It feels like forever as my hand reaches out to grab the door handle and open it.

"What the hell?!" I grunt out as I'm tackled to the ground.

Without thinking about it, I instantly reach up, wrapping my hand around the guy's neck as we roll across the floor, but joke's on me because I find strong fingers grasping my neck in return. Once we smack into the bedframe, the moonlight shines down on us, and I see a flash of light brown eyes. I instantly start cracking up, even if it sounds choked, and loosen my grip from around his neck.

"Damn it, Tey! I could have killed you!" Logan whispers angrily in my face and groans in pain as he rolls to land on his back next to me.

"What a way to go. I always thought I'd die with someone choking me. Either fighting or fucking... maybe both." My grin spreads across my face at the thought.

"You crazy fucker. We need to find Tillie. Now. I got jumped and her soon to be red ass dragged me into the closet even when I told her to run just before I passed out. My fucking head hurts like a bitch," he grinds out through clenched teeth and rolls over to his knees before climbing to his feet slowly.

I'd offer a hand to help, but Logan's pride won't let anyone help him even when he needs it. I jump to my feet and wait by his side just in case he faints, his skin is a little pale around the edges.

"I know. Nicky and I spotted Demon Jokers out front. He's going to take out some of the members we spotted while I came to your rescue, princess." I bow dramatically and quickly stand to dance out of his reach when he growls in anger at my antics.

"How did you guys know to come?" he asked, confused, shaking his head as if to clear it while swaying on his feet.

"Tillie called from your phone. This isn't good, man. I think there's more to the story that we overlooked and messed up big time," I say seriously for the first time ever as I head towards her open bedroom door and peek quickly into the hallway, looking both ways.

It's quiet, the murmur of voices coming from downstairs grows louder at someone yelling the longer we stand here to see if the coast is clear. I almost miss it but my head swings back towards the staircase when I see a shadow move towards the landing.

"We got company. Thirty seconds," I whisper with a hand signal which he ignores as he walks behind her bedroom door while I plaster my body against the wall across from him.

I'm going to take the soon to be dead fucker by surprise. Sneaky is my middle name. Actually, that's a lie. It's Herbert, but I'm taking that to the grave with me. Gotta protect my reputation. The floorboard creaks outside the doorway and a scuffed up boot appears over the threshold. I quickly grab the leather vest and swing the asshole into the room as Logan shuts the door to block out the Demon Joker's surprised shout. Logan kicks behind the club member's knees, making him drop down to the ground with a thud. I wrap my forearm around his throat before he can even recover, my bicep squeezing until he's turning purple in the face.

"How many downstairs?" Logan asks, getting in front of us and nodding at me to loosen my hold slightly so the asshole can talk.

"I ain't tellin' you wannabe thugs shit!" This guy really must be stupid, not seeing the hard, cold look in Logan's eyes.

I swear his normal light brown eyes turn dark, his pupils expanding with his anger climbing at being called a thug. I think the term he should have used is Mafia. Like, show some fucking respect. Logan completely ignores the dry blood sticking to his eyelid from the wound on his head, his gaze focused on the club member with an intensity that makes me raise my brow. This guy might not make it to answering our questions with the way Logan is staring him down. Gone is the cool and collected guy I know, replaced with a furious Logan that hardly ever comes out to play.

"Is Tillie alive? Is she working for you?" Logan's voice comes out raspy and stilted, almost like he didn't want to even ask that last question.

"That cunt?" His laugh comes out dry but cocky and I take a look down at the front of his vest over his shoulder so I can remember his name.

Whiskey... Oh please. Weak ass bitch just likes the drink. He keeps talking even as I tighten my arm around his windpipe in warning. His name is going in my burn book after I kill him. A photo album full of good memories, but bloodier.

"Payne doesn't let his property inside the club business." His words come out taunting as a maniacal smile takes over his face. "Have you been inside her tight pussy? Even when it's dry and bloody, her screams telling us to stop echoes in my ears. Best fuck I've ever had."

Blind rage. That's all I'm feeling. It's like a forbidden door with warning signs swinging open and I'm running through it without looking back. Before Logan can stop me, I release my hold on his throat and grab Whiskey by his chin and wrap my other hand across his forehead to break his fucking neck. The loud, twisted crack is like music to my ears, my own kind of music that only I can understand, making my ears ring for more. I drop his dead body to the floor in disgust, wanting to wash my hands to get the dirty feeling off me. The things he said about our girl... I'm going to kill everyone who's hurt her. I don't care what I have to do. I'll get it done. We all will.

"I'm done with this shit. Did this city forget who the fuck I am? I think it's time we reminded them what exactly we can do. They touched her... Tey, I need you to have my back more than ever tonight, brother." Logan's chest heaves up and down as he bares his teeth at the crumpled body at our feet before sending a swift kick to the corpse of Whiskey.

That seems to calm him down a little bit. He takes a deep breath and pushes his hair off his face until he looks somewhat put together. I hold my fist, bumping his, and nod without saying a word. I have his back no matter what comes our way, always have and always will.

"Let's go save our girl and beg for forgiveness. Nothing hurts her anymore unless it's us." I slap his shoulder and start making my way down the dark hallway towards the stairs.

I don't hear him following but I can feel his menacing presence behind me. The rage is radiating off of him in waves, it feels good to soak those feelings up because it fuels my own. That rage is probably the only thing keeping him from passing out, adrenaline will do that to you too. My phone buzzes in my pocket and when I check the text message flashing on my screen, a grin slips over my lips.

Nicky: Bodies piled out back by the fire pit, going to cause a distraction with some gunpowder. Wait for my signal.

Me: What's the signal? Does it have to do with the corpses you are collecting of club members? That's hot.

Nicky: Let's just say that I'm in a mood to start a bonfire. If you smell burning meat, it's not BBQ. The signal won't be hard to miss, trust me.

Me: Ohhh, keep talking dirty to me. Are we sexting now? Okay, let me have a try. So I just had another man in my arms, whose name was Whiskey. My hand around his throat, I could feel his pulse pounding under my fingertips. I held him real close to my body, gripping him tight... just before I snapped his neck and felt him go limp in my arms. How was that? Turn you on?

Nicky: ... Tey.... just get ready. Focus on Tillie... but tell me more later.

I have to hold back a chuckle as I send him a kissy face emoji and put my phone away in my back pocket. Glancing up, I realize Logan and I are at the bottom of the stairs with his fist clenched on the front of my shirt as he guided me down each step since I was sexting.

Shit.

His face is like thunder as he glances back at me and smacks the back of my head. I easily get distracted but always get the job done at least. My fingers move in random signals, trying to tell Logan what the plan is but he just stares at me before pinching the bridge of his nose. He looks both ways and shoves me across the hall into the living room next to the kitchen.

"What?" he whispers roughly in my ear, patience thin as he peeks around the corner when we hear Diana screeching like a dying pig in a slaughterhouse.

God, she's fucking loud. Hopefully someone duct tapes her lips shut so I can concentrate on killing instead of that awful noise coming out of her mouth.

"Nicky is going to cause a distraction so we have a clear path to get Tillie." I keep my voice low and crouch down by Logan's legs to see what he's looking at.

He doesn't reply, and when I look up at him, his whole body is still. I don't think he's even breathing and that alone tells me I'm not going to like what I see. The moment I look back down and glance around the corner, I have to bite down on my knuckle to contain the snarl that climbs up my throat. I take in everything at once. There's a gun at Diana's temple as she struggles in a club member's arms, his patch on his vest over his pec indicates that his name is Poe. I couldn't care less if she dies. My main focus is on Dalton and the stab wound in his stomach that is bleeding in a steady flow. I can't tell if he's breathing from here, he's not even moving, his still form slumped motionless in the chair. I almost miss it but I catch his arm muscles shifting. My gaze goes straight to the windows behind him to see his fingers moving in the reflection of the glass as he works on those knots of rope around his wrist. I didn't realize I was holding my breath. Knowing he's alive makes the tightness in my chest ease, but not a moment later, that tightness is back when I hear her, my heart stopping at the sound.

"No. No. No. No." Tillie keeps muttering the word under her ragged breath and I'm almost scared to look at her to figure out why her voice comes out desperately broken and lost.

My hand grabs for my knife before I realize what I'm doing, ready to fling it across the room at one of the two fuckers holding her down. Logan grasps my wrist before I can send the blade flying and shakes his head silently without even glancing down at me. I look at Tillie and back at Logan, feeling my body vibrating with the need to do something, anything. Logan's eyes are veiled, his gaze unblinking as he stares at the back of Franco's head that's currently between Tillie's legs. I've never had respect for Franco but never really had thoughts of killing him either. Okay, that's a lie. I daydream of killing all the time and he's been in a few of those fantasies but the urge to rip his throat out with my bare hands right here, right now, is unbelievably strong for daring to eat my girl out.

No one can see us, all their attention on Tillie as she trembles like a baby deer under Payne's relentless, tight hold. I recognize him from all the photos Nicky uploaded on his computer as he's been digging into the club business and Tillie's background. This is her dad. Her fucking dad holding a gun towards Dalton as he laughs and watches her stepdad go down on her.

"You're going to come all over his tongue or I'll put a bullet through lover boy's head over here." Payne waves his gun threateningly in a gleeful tone and makes Tillie spread her legs wider by kicking her feet farther apart with his boot.

I don't think she hears him, her eyes are hazy like she's not really here but she whimpers and pinches her eyes closed as her body starts to shake under Franco's tongue. The fucker's not even pretending to not enjoy her pussy, he's practically a starving man as he laps at her lower lips.

She's going to come whether she wants to or not. Her head is telling her no, the one word she keeps chanting, but she doesn't have control of her body.

"He's dead to me," Logan hisses through his clenched teeth and I know he's talking about Franco.

There's a difference between being forced to do something and wanting to. The way Franco groans and picks up speed on her clit tells me he's happy right where he is. I'm going to cut out his tongue and shove it up his ass. I don't fucking care that he's built his own empire, a Don to his mafia, and has hundreds of followers. I'll be there when he takes his last breath. That's a promise I intend to keep for hurting my angel.

Logan's whole body shakes with uncontrollable anger and he moves out from behind our hiding spot before Nicky can even give us the signal. So much for the plan, but I can't sit back and watch any more of this without doing something either.

"You have one second to get your hand off my girl or fucking die," Logan says in a deadly calm voice as he steps into the light of the kitchen.

All heads turn our way but Franco's as I stand next to Lo with my arms crossed, pretending to be bored even though I'm all pent-up with the urge to murder. I notice Tillie's whole body sinks in Payne's hold like she can't hold herself up anymore, relieved that someone is here for her.

Has no one ever been there for her? Well, that's about to change.

"Ah, this must be the son." Payne looks at Logan with a raised brow and dismisses him easily like he's not a threat.

Wrong move. Logan's the animal you don't see coming until it strikes, a monster that's going to enjoy tearing Payne apart, limb by limb.

Franco glances over his shoulder, wiping his gleaming lips on the shoulder of his fancy jacket as he looks at Logan with eyes void of any emotion.

"Logan." Franco slowly rises to his feet with his lip curling into a satisfied smirk with cold, dead eyes.

My best friend takes a threatening step forward. I'm not sure if he planned to go for the Demon Jokers' president or his father, but glass shattering from the French doors on the other side of the kitchen causes us to all duck. Guess we'll never know who would have been on the receiving end of Logan's punishing and murdering intent due to Nicky's distraction. I didn't know he could make a small bomb out of gunpowder, color me surprised when he can make something explode out of something so small and simple. I guess a bonfire turns into a fourth of July firework show when it comes to Nicky...Show-off. The heat of the fire pit blazes so high into the night sky that I can even feel the warmth of the fire from here. I jump into action just as an anguished roar echoes around the kitchen. Dalton tears out of the rope like the hulk and takes off at a run to tackle Poe to the ground in a football move that would even impress a college scout. Diana goes flying off somewhere, but I'm already leaping across the kitchen island to land right by Tillie. I don't have any flying fucks to give what happens to her mother, she can fend for herself for all I care. I catch Tillie as her legs collapse and quickly guide her out of harm's way as Logan fights with Payne for the gun.

"You motherfucker! You dare to put your hands on what's mine!" Logan bellows, delivering a swift punch to Payne's kidney that has him keeling over with a grunt of pain.

Franco just stands there, fixing his suit jacket so it's straight then bends down to grab the gun that slides across the floor at his feet. Looks like Dalton got the weapon out of Poe's hold, and it sounds like he's going to town punching the club member with his big fists. Maybe beating him to death, I want to watch but my gaze is locked on Franco as he calmly lifts the gun and pulls the trigger. Tillie jerks in my hold as blood splashes against us both like a warm shower spray. Her body goes stiff as she watches Logan slump against the cabinet and wipes blood from his upper lip as he breathes hard.

"No! What have you done?!" Tillie screams hysterically, her voice hoarse as she struggles in my hold like a wildcat.

She slips out of my hands before I can stop her and drops to her knees beside Payne. My angel gazes down at him with tears streaking down her beautiful face, looking at the perfect bullet hole between Payne's eyes. She makes a fist and brings it down onto the once President of a motorcycle club's chest. Tillie does it again, harder this time until she's using both hands and screaming out like a broken animal. I stare at her, knowing this has nothing to do with the pain of losing someone you love.

"Baby girl," Logan whispers and wipes the splattered blood off his hands before wiping a tear off her cheek with his thumb.

"No!" She swats his hand away and shakily climbs to her feet, turning towards Franco as she sobs uncontrollably. "You had no right! It was supposed to be me! His death was going to be by my hands!" Her voice comes out shaky and defeated, but the look she gives Franco is the strongest I've ever seen her.

Rage shines in her tear-filled eyes, even as she chokes on her sobs, she swings back her arm and slaps Franco with everything she has before I can stop her.

His head whips to the side, a red handprint darkening his cheek and he rubs a hand over the spot as he glances back at Tillie with hard eyes. I don't like that look in his gaze that's a mix between fury and lust, it has me stepping over Payne's body to pull her into my body and away from him as she goes limp like everything that's happened is hitting her at once.

"I'll let it slide this one time, little girl. You have a week to get yourself together and then come back home by your own will or by my hand," Franco orders darkly and strides over to Diana, gripping her by the elbow to drag her shaking body out of the room without looking back.

I don't bother looking at anyone, I know Logan will look after Dalton as I take care of our girl. I pick Tillie up, cradling her in my arms, and hold her close to my chest. Walking over the shattered glass and through the French doors, I keep going until I'm sinking into the warm shallow end of the pool. I don't care if my clothes get wet, the only thing that matters is healing my Angel who hasn't said one word to me or protested my actions. She lays her cheek against my chest, inhaling a shaky breath as I switch her position so her legs can wrap around my waist. She lets me walk us deeper into the water until it starts turning a bright red against the light blue water. Her father's blood washes off our bodies, leaving behind the smell of chlorine instead of the strong scent of copper. I don't glance over as a shadow falls above us, staying silent as he watches us from the edge of the pool. Not even a minute later, a small splash beside us lets me know he is done waiting. My eyes meet Nicky's over Tillie's shoulder when he steps closer and moves her hair off of her shoulder. She doesn't move, just stares off in the distance and sinks into my body as Nicky steps up behind her back. He places his chin on her shoulder, sliding his arms around until I feel his hands grip my waist and just holds her tightly between our bodies until there's hardly room to breathe.

"We got you," I whisper down at her and cradle her closer just so I know she's really in my arms.

CHAPTER 3

Tillie

I'm warm, cocooned in a dream of heat. Maybe a little too warm. My clothes stick to my body like a second skin. I try to roll away from the constant heat to cool down but something stops me from moving.

Holding me hostage.

I blink my eyes open, only to see my feet dangling inches from the cold, cement flooring as my chin drops towards my chest. A red trail of blood slides down my legs, dripping to the floor like a teardrop and leaving a small puddle underneath me. The strain in my shoulders suddenly becomes so overwhelming that I jerk my head up, an agonizing hiss leaving my mouth as I take in my wrists chained to the ceiling. I sway from side to side so slowly that it makes me nauseous. It doesn't help that I'm in pain and bleeding from the deep cuts on my wrists from the metal cuffs. How long have I been hanging here? Unbelievable, intense heat settles against my back, leaving behind the smell of burnt flesh. A scream rips out of my throat, the sound soul-stirring even to my own ears, and a noise I hope to never hear again. I'm thrashing to get away, but the heat stops sizzling as whatever burns me is pulled away. My body slumps in the shackles, and the breath whooshing in and out of me is loud and hard.

"*Do you really want to know? What will you give me in*

return?" Payne's voice comes from beside my right ear, a whisper of a ghost haunting me.

Dark, dirty, biker boots stop in front of my swaying body as I remain silent and a deeply tanned hand lifts my chin so I'm staring into eyes that make me feel like I'm looking into the abyss of hell.

My own personal hell.

"You're dead." The words leave my panting lips, terror nearly making me pass out as he finally steps into my line of sight.

"Am I? I'll always be here, Tillie." He taps my head with his knuckle and chuckles at my expression that has likely gone pale. "Aren't you going to ask? I know you're dying to know. You can't help yourself." He shakes his head when tears pool in my eyes because I know exactly what he's talking about but I can't play this game anymore.

There's only so much I can take and I'm not ready for this moment that will change everything I thought I knew. I lick my dry, cracked lips and stare over his shoulder at the workbench that holds all my worst nightmares. This isn't right. I remember this moment, the first time I was brought down to the basement with endless days of pain inflicted on my body at the age of sixteen. Except this memory is different, Payne never offered an explanation as to why he wanted to hurt me. I never got my answer but I think I finally understand why he tortured me for countless hours.

"What do you want?" I choke back a sob, despising myself when I can't help but glance back at him and hating the evil smile that spreads across his lips at my desperate tone.

"I want you to suffer but first I want you to ask me. Go ahead and ask me!" He suddenly screams the last part in my face, his spittle landing on my cheeks from how close he is to me. He's so close that I can't see anything but his harsh, brown eyes.

"Who is my father?" I breathe out in a strangled, raspy tone while staring into his eyes that hide many secrets and will continue to, just to see me suffer.

He stares at me for an amount of time that feels like forever *before he turns around and starts walking away into the dark void. At the edge of where dark and light meets, he stops next to a man with his back towards me. The patch of the Demon Jokers stares at me and Payne places his arm around the man's shoulder, leading him away and into the dark.*

"No! You can't do this! Who is he?!" My shouting echoes all around me, and I yank on my wrists so hard that they burn from the pressure.

"I think you already know the answer to that, Tillie," Payne says over his shoulder and continues walking into the shadows with the man until they are only a body outline with little light, being swallowed up by the black abyss.

"Look at me! goddammit, look at me!" I scream with every-thing inside of me, fighting against my restraints to break free, to run to them, but it's no use.

The man never looks back, the last thing I see is the dancing demon with a joker's mask over its face on the back of his vest. I'm left alone with a single lightbulb swinging over my head. The screams don't stop leaving my mouth, even when my throat hurts.

"Come back," I whisper brokenly on a sob.

"Tillie! Wake the fuck up! Come on, little bitch, don't do this!"

My body jerks like it's been struck by lightning as I struggle to sit up. Hands restrain my wrists as I take deep, gasping breaths and fight against the body looming over my own.

"Fuck, Tillie. It's me. It's Dalton," the gravelly, deep voice whispers in my ear with a ragged breath as if he's been running for miles.

My blurry, watery eyes blink rapidly until Dalton's face over mine comes into focus. It's like the fight goes out of my body as I collapse against the mattress. Dalton relaxes his tense muscles along with mine as he exhales a relieved breath.

"What happened? Wh–where are we?" I croak out in a stutter, taking stock of my surroundings as my brain battles against sleep and being woken up.

I'm laying on a bed with a navy blue comforter, and tan walls surround the small room with a bathroom door slightly open, the light inside it on. A dresser and nightstand are the only other items in the room that tell me nothing. It gives away nothing of where I am and whose bedroom I am in, but then the smell of gasoline and cedar fills my senses and tells me this is Dalton's room.

"Welcome to Hell's Devils. I don't remember much after passing out on Logan's kitchen floor but he got a hold of our Hell's Devils doc just for this kind of situation and brought him here to the compound." His violet gaze flickers between mine, his massive arms on either side of my head once he lets go of my wrists.

My gaze drops to his naked torso, taking in the white bandage wrapped around his tapered waist. I can't stop my hand from trembling as I graze my fingers over the spot he was stabbed. He could have died. The thought hits me hard, making a shaky breath get stuck in the back of my throat as my eyes water.

"This is my fault," I whisper, feeling just as evil as Payne for the first time in my life.

Dalton grunts and moves off of me to roll carefully on his side so he can stare into my eyes as we lay side by side. For a club of dangerous motorcycle gang members, the compound is eerily quiet. It's the type of silence that comes with a death and that hollow feeling grows in my chest because of his dad… that's my fault too.

"Shut up. So expressive." He drags his thumb along my cheekbone as he looks deep into my eyes before leaning forward to place his forehead against mine with a deep sigh.

"I'm sorry, little bitch," he whispers so softly, that nickname starting to sound like an endearment to me.

I rear my head back, startled, and shake my head. "You're sorry? Everything that's happened has been my fault from the moment I stepped foot in Logan's house. I should have disappeared where no one could find me but instead, I stayed out in the open where people I care about got hurt."

I can't even look at him, guilt laying heavy on my chest. I'm already thinking of an escape out of this town...This state. I'm going to always be running while looking over my shoulder, but at least the guys won't get hurt anymore because of me. Dalton huffs out an angry breath and grasps my chin with his thumb and index finger so that I have no choice but to look at him.

"You care about me? Fuck, Tillie. After everything we've done and what has happened to you..." His jaw goes tight as he glances at the ceiling and lays on his back instead of looking at me. "I don't even know how you can stand the sight of me."

I stare at his side profile; the sharp edges of his jawline, the high cheekbones on his honey golden skin, and the long dark lashes that frame his beautiful purple, brown eyes.

"I like a little pain in my life, Dalton. It's all I've ever known. I couldn't figure it out at first, the attraction I felt for you guys. Even when you kept pushing me, forcing me to my knees, controlling my body... everything you guys did and still do makes me want you. Maybe it's the desire to have someone who is just as broken as me. It could be because I can see that I wasn't the only one thrust into this life and seeing the family you guys are, willing to go to any length to protect each other... I've never had that and I want that. *Need* that. I stayed to seek revenge, at least, that's what I told myself, but deep down I want what you guys have. A family to fight for," I admit in a quiet voice and hold his gaze when he finally looks back at me.

"I don't know how to make this right? I've done, and probably will continue to do, things that will hurt you," he says, expanding his massive chest on an exhale, and the look on his face... he looks so lost.

"Do you want me, Dalton?" I make sure to not break eye contact, even though I'm feeling exposed.

"Desperately so, little bitch," he answers right away, no hesitation.

He knows, he knows my deepest secret. I'm broken, scared, and damaged, but for some reason, he still wants me.

"Everyone has always wanted something from me but not desperately." I offer a tiny smile before sitting up in bed and stretching my arms over my head.

My whole body feels stiff like I haven't moved in days and I wonder how long we've been holed up in his room. Where are the rest of the guys? I scoot over the side of the bed and stand, making my way over to his bathroom because I'm pretty sure I have a case of bedhead. A shower sounds perfect before I have to leave the safety of his room to face reality. Just a few more minutes.

"I'll prove to you how much I need you," he says across the room in that gravelly voice that sends pleasant chills down my spine.

He needs me?

I pivot around on my heels to face him just as I step into the bathroom doorway and squeal in surprise at finding him so close behind me. I didn't even hear him move, especially for someone so big and wounded.

"Jesus! Make some noise would you? What are you doing?" I raise a brow as he keeps stepping forward until I have no choice but to keep moving backwards.

My lower back bumps against the edge of the bathroom

counter and I just stand there with my mouth dropping open as he begins to unwrap the binding around his waist. He reaches over without looking and turns on the shower, holding my gaze the whole time. Almost like a challenge glittering in his eyes.

"Get undressed," he orders, a small smirk forming on his plush lips as I place my fists on my hips.

"How about no?" I sass back and jump with a shriek as he moves real fast and cages me against the sink.

"How about yes and don't argue with me. I'm just going to take care of you. Besides, you kind of stink." He says this while rubbing his nose along mine and winks.

I would hit him, but the teasing light in his eyes makes me give in to his demands. Challenge accepted. He'll just have to suffer being naked in a closed space with me without touching. It's his own fault anyways.

"How long was I out for? I don't remember anything after being in the pool." I keep my gaze down as I start to take my clothes off, biting my lip because I'm not quite ready to talk about Payne fully.

"Just two days. You needed it. Doc gave you something to help you sleep and I felt better having you by my side while getting stitched up." He waves to the stitches on his lower stomach when I take a peek from under my lashes. The slash isn't big and I'm happy it didn't seem to hit anything major.

"Are you in pain right now?" I whisper, crossing my arms over my naked chest as I bite my lip so I don't start crying again.

I'm so tired of crying. I used to think that all my tears were dried up because no matter how sad I was, I couldn't cry. Now it's like I can't stop, years of built up sorrow and pain pours out of me. Tears cascade down my cheeks, set off without my control and I don't know when I'll be able to stop crying. I hate it.

"No, little bitch. I'm fine, I've had worse. It's just a flesh wound and it only looked bad because I lost some blood. Get in the shower." He holds the door open and reaches for my hand with his palm facing up for me to grab.

I almost wish he would go back to his loving, jerk self, this is almost too much to handle. He's being nice, it does put me on edge a little bit because it's hard to trust that someone has good intentions towards me. With a small head shake to get rid of those thoughts, I hesitantly place my hand in his and it doesn't go unnoticed but he doesn't say a word. The moment the hot water hits my back, I'm gone. Completely gone. My body gradually starts to relax, my head falling back under the spray as it soaks my hair. A sigh of bliss escapes my parted lips as hot water seeps into my skin and I didn't even realize my eyes slid shut until Dalton coughs in the open stall doorway. Peeking through slitted eyes, I gaze at him as he just stands there. His eyes travel unhurriedly over my body, like he has all the time in the world as he looks me up and down before finally looking into my eyes with hunger burning in his gaze. My breath catches in the back of my throat at the way he's looking at me. He sees all my scars on display, each tattoo trying to cover a part of my past and he's already dived into a part of myself that I keep hidden. He knows almost everything that has happened to me but still, his gaze could set this whole bathroom on fire from the burning desire in his violet eyes.

"You are the most beautiful fucking thing I've ever seen. Do you know how much I want you? It's pure torture looking at you, needing to touch you and lose myself inside you. You're the only thing holding me together right now, Tillie. I need to make this right, tell me how and I'll do whatever you ask." His voice goes rough, deeper.

A man like Dalton, his big muscles and charming white smile can get him anything he wants. He knows this and has used it to his advantage. I've seen it firsthand the very first day I met him when Mrs. Sullivan was on her knees for him, knowing the risk of getting caught. The risk was worth it. *He* is worth it.

I gaze down at his body, seeing his cock incredibly hard and thick. So hard that it almost looks painful. The vein that runs from base to tip throbs as I stare, his monster cock jerks and leaks a pearl of cum from his big, fat mushroom head. I honestly don't know how that thing fits into my body, but my pussy clenches in need to have it again, sliding roughly in and out of me. I can handle the pain, the stretch as he pushes his huge cock in my tight pussy, hammering into me like he doesn't plan on ever stopping but the endless pleasure is worth it all.

"Whatever I ask?" I lick my lips and glance up into his eyes as he stares down at me, placing my hand over his pounding heart.

"Anything," He rasps out, that smile widening on his sexy lips like he can read my mind.

"You're going to fuck me and fuck me often." I quickly place my finger over his lips when he starts to open his mouth and his eyes heat. "But you can't come. Not until I say you're allowed to."

His eyes widen in shock as I drop my finger from his lips and it takes a lot out of me to not smile. He looks like I just kicked his puppy or stabbed him. I've seen his face when he was stabbed and even then his face didn't look this pale.

"You're serious?" He squeezes his eyes closed and swallows thickly but glances back at me and then down at his dick with a sad expression. "I'm sorry, man, but if this proves to her that we aren't going anywhere then it's just you and my hand for now on until we get the green light."

I've never seen a man talk to his penis before like a close friend but that body part is pretty important so I guess it makes sense. He's in for a rude awakening though. I almost feel bad but not really.

"No." I shake my head at him and his brows wrinkle in confusion.

"What?" he asks warily, like he's almost afraid of my answer.

"You don't get to come, Dalton, even with your own hand. I'm the only one who can take your pleasure. Me. Not Tey, not Nicky, not Logan, and definitely not even yourself." I'm not sure why my voice comes out husky but it does.

Knowing that only I can give and take away his pleasure sends a thrill through me. It's something I've never had and I really want him to do this. It will prove to me that he does want me enough. Dalton is a man of carnal desire, pleasure, and I'm about to take that away from him.

He scrubs a hand down his face and curses before looking at his cock again with a pained expression. It takes a second, but he finally glances back at me with the most serious face I've ever seen on him.

"Whatever it takes. I'll be in constant pain but you're fucking worth it." He doesn't waste a second more and pulls me into his arms while I rest my head over his hard pec.

"You're going to suffer terribly," I mutter against his skin.

"I'm already suffering but trust me, little bitch. Give this a chance. Give *me* a chance," he mutters against the top of my head as he rests his cheek there and tightens his hold around me.

"It won't be easy for me but something tells me you guys are worth it."

"You want all of us?" he questions slowly and pulls back to look down at me, his eyes wide with disbelief and he shakes his head in wonder as he palms the side of my face.

"Well, my plan was to make you all jealous and fight over me, but I learned that you guys share almost everything. So that plan went down the drain. You all have beautiful cocks even when you're forcing them down my throat. I can't help but want more." I shrug and he chuckles before settling his lips softly against mine for a second before groaning as if in pain.

"Why do I have a feeling my punishment isn't the worst compared to Logan, Nicky, and Tey?" He laughs harder at the smirk forming on my lips and I pretend to zip my mouth closed before throwing away the key.

He shakes his head and reaches around me to grab his body wash, chuckling every few seconds as if the thought of his friends being punished by me is amusing to him. He starts to slide his big hands along my collarbone before moving down lower with another pained groan as he lathers the slippery suds all over my breasts.

"Fuck. You're an evil woman but I like that," he says as he continues to soap me up without once trying to tempt me with his massive, magic dick.

This might work but then again, maybe I'm punishing myself too.

Only time will tell.

CHAPTER 4

Dalton

"**D**id you hear me, Prez?" The sound of Tank's voice brings me out from the brink of drowning in my grief.

It's been three days. Three days since I found out my old man was murdered. That the girl I want to keep by my side was brutally raped by the Demon Jokers, her *Father* threw her to the wolves. And now I'm sitting in my dad's chair at the head of the table with a new patch over my vest that says President. It doesn't feel real. I keep pressing on the stitches on my stomach to make sure I'm actually awake. It helps but doesn't at the same time. This isn't supposed to be my chair for years to come but here I am and planning a war at that. The club trusted Pike with their lives and didn't hesitate to vote me as their new President before my father's skin was cold.

I feel like shit, probably look like it too but the church meeting is urgent. Believe me when I wish I could be locked upstairs in my room with Tillie and hide from all my new responsibilities. The wicked don't rest and my brothers in arms are hungry for vengeance.

"No. Sorry, brother. Continue." I scrub my hand down my face roughly and try to harden my heart.

Maybe when this shit storm is clear, I might have time to grieve but for now, I have to lock away those feelings. I can't even catch my breath for one goddamn second. That's how it goes when you sign up for this lifestyle, it's always something.

"I had Gunnar gift wrap Payne's head in a box and will have it delivered along with his members to the Demon Jokers' doorstep. I expect retaliation since it was their president and to be honest, I'm looking forward to it." Tank leans back in his chair with his arms crossed and his gaze distant.

I wasn't here when our charter was attacked, half the club wasn't. It was a Sunday evening and most of the guys went home to their families or with some tail for the night. Only a few were left hanging around the compound including my old man. No one saw the attack from the Demon Jokers coming. Tank was just rolling up to the gates on his motorcycle and heard a rumble of bikes down the street. He could make out the Joker patch on the back of their vests and he didn't even wait for the gate to open all the way before he was hopping off his bike. He was greeted with blood smeared along the bar and five of our men dead. My dad, his president, died in his arms. My dad's last words were to Tank when they should have been for my ears only. I haven't asked what he said, I'm not ready.

Tank has been quiet and right by my side since I took over. He's kept our brothers from seeking out revenge without a plan. He's kept everyone calm while I've been trying to wrap my head around everything that has happened. I made him Vice President without a second thought.

"Payne has probably already been replaced so we'll be ready for when they come. Nicky and Tey didn't get much information out of the west side gang member but this isn't our first run-in with them. Looks like the Los Muerte is now in alliance with the Demon Jokers and someone else in our fucking city. Right under our noses, but they can't hide forever. We'll find out who it is." I look at my members around our oval table, each of their expressions ranging from pissed off to downright vile.

We all want blood to spill but we are going to do it my way.

"It's because of that girl, isn't it? We have the enemy's daughter under our fucking roof and just letting her roam around as she pleases. We should be sending them her head along with her dear old dad." Axel slams his fist down on the table, his face turning red as he tries to stare me down.

I don't say anything, my face stays blank the longer I look at him until he glances away first under my stare.

"You touch a hair on her head and I won't hesitate to skin you alive after boiling you in hot water so each strip of skin I peel off comes away like butter. You understand me, *brother*?" I snarl the last word in sarcasm, leaning forward in my seat without looking away from him as he gazes around at everyone else.

They won't be helping him. I wear the motherfucking patch that says where I belong.

"I hear ya, Prez." Axel clears his throat and glares straight ahead at nothing.

"Good. I'll address this once and we move forward with plans." I pause, making sure I have everyone's attention. "Tillie is my old lady from this day forward and she will be wearing my name. She may have come from the Demon Jokers charter but Payne wasn't her biological father. It's not my story to tell but I will say she's a victim and was never treated like a club member. Whoever is siding with those bastards and feeding them information will die very fucking soon. Los Muerte knew who she was at first glance as they'd been looking for her since the moment she stepped foot in California. Payne had word out he was looking for Tillie but she was found too easily and too soon if you get my drift.

Someone is feeding information and I will be finding out who." My voice comes out harsh, my teeth grinding because I will find the fucker who keeps putting our girl in trouble.

The leather of my vest squeaks as I shift in my seat and place my elbows on the table as I glance each member in the eye. A few nod, some grunt in acknowledgment, and I relax slightly from my stiff posture knowing that I have them in agreement with me.

Maybe I can do this. If I have the numbers to back me up, we can get our revenge and I'll be able to run Hell's Devils.

"Where do you want us?" Diesel questions, giving me a slight nod in respect.

"I want all ears to the ground and we'll wait until we hear what the new president of the Demon Jokers has to say. I want more patrols on the compound and bikes on the road. If you see any of the west side Los Muerte, catch them and bring them to the warehouse." In old fashion, I pick up the gavel that's been used for every church meeting and slam it down once in dismissal.

Chairs screech on the wood floor as members stand and file out the doors until it's just me and Tank left in the room.

"Axel might be a problem but I'll keep an eye out on him." Tank rubs his beard, lost in thought before he shakes his head. "How's it going with your *old lady*?" He air quotes with a chuckle as I heave a sigh and drop back into my chair with a groan.

How's it going? I've got fucking blue balls. I wouldn't be surprised if they fell off because she's fucking torturing me. Bending this way and that way with her peachy ass right in front of my face basically. The little she-devil knows exactly what she's doing. I can do this. For her, I'll pick my cold, lonely, blue balls off the floor and lock them away until I can earn her trust and she gives me the green light.

"It's, uh, going, to say the least. Driving me crazy but

nothing I can't handle," I say out loud, running my hand through my hair as I try to gather my thoughts.

"You know what they say about the crazy ones, right?" Tank says with a serious, straight face as I raise a brow for him to continue. "Animals in the sack, man. Scratching claws, squeezes a man with a death grip of that sweet pussy as she rides you off into the sunset."

He rubs a hand off his lips to hide his smile as I glare at him. Just the thought of Tillie and her pussy on any other man's mind besides my friends has me seeing red.

"Anyone touches her... their body will never be found." My words come out strained, almost growling as I bare my teeth at him.

Tank holds his hands out in a calming gesture but fights a smile once more as he opens his mouth. "No one's going to even think about touching her, man. You know the code. Old ladies are off-limits."

My mood sours even more, just the thought of how many men have touched her skin without her permission makes me want to destroy everything in my path. I don't feel guilty about having her lips wrapped around my cock that one night in the garage, forcing her to her knees without asking. I saw fire in her gaze, it almost burnt me and I needed that directed fully on me because I feel fucking alive with just one look from her. She was beautiful stealing the Ferrari, and coming at us with each step of her long, toned legs as she stood up to us. I've never had a woman look at me with an unhinged gaze like she couldn't decide if she wanted to cut off my cock or jump on it.

Of course, I took that from her choice and fed her every single inch of my cock. She was staring up at me, us, with hate but that didn't stop her from licking our dicks like it was the best flavored ice cream she's ever had. I really needed to stop thinking about her perfect lips and my cock all in one sentence. My blood tends to rush straight down to my prized possession and is twitching in seconds with the urge to claim her pussy until the only weeping my little bitch is doing is that sweet honey between her legs.

My eyes squeeze shut as the memory of her wide, scared, tear-filled eyes looked at me as that dipshit, Franco, spread her pussy lips and ate her out like she was his. I want to murder him, bury him somewhere far out in the desert where I can visit just to piss on his grave. The only thing stopping me is Logan... and Dom. Everything he said at his rave has been playing in my head since then on repeat. I don't like the guy and his cocky attitude but even my old man was suspicious of Franco and Jin for years. Didn't trust them.

I shake my head to clear my thoughts and stand up, reaching for my phone in my back pocket as it buzzes once.

"Just keep an eye out, brother, and spread the word that no one touches my property," I order over my shoulder and receive one single nod from Tank just as I walk out the doors leading into the main part of the compound.

Passing the bar with a few club members sitting around and some low music of rock and roll playing on the speakers, I swipe my phone open and freeze at the image that pops on my screen.

I stop dead in my tracks and blink a few times just to make sure I'm seeing things right.

Unknown number: You don't deserve my queen. Can you really keep her safe?

The image takes my breath away to say the least. I'm fucking pissed... furious but I can admire a good photo when I see one. She's stunning and it kills me every single time I look at her.

Tillie is in a dressing room, her back turned towards the camera and her head bent down as she touches the white, silk bow just below her belly button. She doesn't notice Dom behind her in the mirror as she tries on lingerie.

Dalton: You're a dead man walking. I'm her fucking Daddy and I swear to God if she calls you Papi again because you provoked her...

I jam out that text quickly, surprised my screen doesn't crack and glance up to notice everyone left in the bar area staring at me like I'm a caged animal at a circus. My other hand grips the sides of my head, pulling strands of my hair in frustration and I'm breathing pretty hard like I just ran miles.

The sound of my fist slamming into the wall next to the staircase has the club whore squeaking behind the bar as she shatters a glass.

"Round the fuck up!" I roar and stomp up the stairs in a rush towards my room, ignoring the sound of rushing feet and barstools tipping over downstairs.

I basically kick my door down and glance around frantically just in case the photo was some other woman that happens to look a fuck ton like Tillie. I know that's not possible because no one has a bubbly ass like hers and I'd recognize it anywhere. Finding my room empty just confirmed she's really not here. I know she's been going stir-crazy up in my room, but I just wanted to keep her safe and away from my club brothers for a little bit. So much for that, because now I'm going to be introducing her to everyone all at once. I'm taking every single body available to go search for her.

My phone pings again and I grind my teeth in frustration as I stomp out of my room while heading back downstairs towards the machine shop where my bike is stored.

Logan: What the fuck! Why isn't she at the club?!

Tey: Think she's trying on that little outfit for us? I think red silk would look better on my sugar plum's sweet, delicious body just like blood but I'm not complaining. Also, can we kill him now?

Nicky: Already hacking into her phone location. Text you the coordinates in a sec.

I wait for what feels like forever for him to give us her location. The sound of grumbling bike engines and the Hell's Devils stomping of feet over asphalt makes it slightly easier to breathe because that means my club members are ready to ride out.

Nicky: SeaSide Mall. Meet you guys there in ten minutes. Also, I call dibs on spanking her ass for this.

I swing my leg over my motorcycle and ride it to a crawl towards the front until two rows of thirty badass bikers are at my back. Fuck, this is hard. My dad used to ride front and center while I was to his right behind him. At least I have the manpower to kick some ass if anything goes sideways. I grab my shades out of my vest pocket and signal with my hand to get moving just as my bike glides onto the road.

My little bitch is in so much trouble when I get my hands on her. My palm is already twitching.

CHAPTER 5

Dom

I can't remember the last time I was in a mall. I think it was a long time ago, before I took over for my father, before my mother ran away from this life by filling up her bathroom with red marks where I found her. Jagged lines on her wrists and open, glazed eyes that stared blankly back at me. I think that was the last day I had any freedom to be a normal kid, as normal as any kid growing up in the Cartel can get. Drugs, a suicidal mother, and a father that ruled his cocaine kingdom with an iron fist until the day he was shot down. I should be back at the estate, running my numbers and shipments for the next supply of weed coming in from my fields in Mexico but instead, I'm at the fucking SeaSide Mall following my future queen around.

I'd usually be at one of the facilities, watching over my army of working men, seeing the comings and goings, or even testing the supply. I have the best marijuana on the streets, across the whole country, and most are gunning for my spot. I guess I'm like my father, in the way I don't trust easily, never will and I oversee everything instead of letting someone else do my work. This is my life but damn if it isn't a lonely one. My schedule changed about a week ago in the dark tunnels, the atmosphere high on drugs of bliss and sex. I've been waiting years for that day to look Logan Russo in his eyes and turn his whole world upside down by the information I've collected over the years but that all stopped once she looked at me. Dark, haunted eyes that's seen too much push to the surface. She tries to bury it all deep down, but hurt bleeds out of her soul and touches mine with just one connection of our gazes. Don't even get me started on her body that is made to sin and tempt a man of faith to his knees before her just so he can have a taste.

Usually, a pressed suit is molded to my body but my choices for the day are all black clothing for stalking. Black jeans and a black leather jacket with the hoodie pulled up to cover my face as I stalk behind Tillie without her knowledge. I've had my men watching the Hell's Devils compound for days since I've found out she's transferred there instead of the Russo mansion. I'm not complaining about her staying at the compound, anywhere is safer for her but at that fucking house of the devil. Most nights after a really long day, I'd change into clothes that blend into the night and watch across the street from the motorcycle club for any sign of her.

Every. Single. Night.

Luck was on my side today when I got a call from Zeus that my queen was sneakily climbing over a fence and hopping into a jeep with Nicky's little sister only for them to end up at the mall. Cutting all my meetings short, and delaying a shipment coming in from the docks, I changed and here I am a few paces behind her, stalking slowly through the crowded mall without her knowing that someone is watching and following her every move. A few times her shoulders have gone tight and she pauses in the middle of the crowds to look around her like she can feel me watching her.

At first, I was fucking pissed that she was out without one of the guys with her, unprotected with Nicholas' little sister but she isn't clueless. I see the way she looks people in the eye so she remembers their faces, scanning her surroundings even though she's laughing at whatever her friend says. She's smart, cunning, and drop dead gorgeous. There's more to her than meets the eyes and that is what has me obsessed. Can't say I've ever had to stalk a woman before, usually they end up in my bed before I even get home. I snap my fingers and can have any woman on their knees at a moment's notice but something in the way Tillie holds her chin up and glares tells me she's not one to go on her knees willingly without a fight. She has fire and I want to be burned by her.

"Oh! Let's go in there! Butt licker! Out of our way!" Nicola shouts at the top of her lungs without a care in the world as she shoves through a group of leering males, pulling on Tillie's hand towards the lingerie store.

I like little Nicholas' sister too. She's good for Tillie, makes her laugh, and smiles a real smile instead of something forced. I'll let Nicola live just for that alone.

I follow close behind but far enough that they don't notice me as I duck into a nearby shop until they go deeper into the store. Stepping into the path of the men that are elbowing each other and still looking where my queen entered, I lift my face and make sure they can see I'm staring at each of them. They say my face is something that resembles an angel with my good looks and sharp edges but what they don't know is that even Lucifer fell from the heavens. Tempted with dark looks and even darker eyes that smacked the fear into anyone who looked into his gaze.

You're playing a game with the devil, and I love my games.

"Mine."

It's the only word I say in a deep tone, my dark gaze connecting with each of them. There must be that look in my eyes that say I will fucking kill you and there won't be a body to find because two of them gulp audibly while the other one holds up his hands, backing up slowly.

"Yeah, yeah, man. Yours," he quickly says and nudges his friends to get moving.

They turn in the other direction, practically running. I can smell their fear from a mile away, I love stalking and playing into people's fears. It makes them prey while the wolf hunts them down to tear a big bite into their skin, eating until there's nothing left.

With a pleased, dark chuckle, I walk casually into the lingerie shop with my hands in my pockets and try not to imagine what Tillie would look like in a pair of white lace underwear, appearing from the fucking heavens just like the angel that she is.

I trail behind her slowly, making sure my body is turned sideways from her in case she happens to glance in my direction. She's distracted though, gliding her slim fingers over lingerie as she walks by but never picks out anything.

"Can I help you, sir?" a breathy female voice asks from right next to me, I roll my eyes and ignore her since she's been following me the moment I stepped in the store.

I don't bother glancing at the employee as I watch Tillie head into the back of the store, staring longingly at every item she passes. I wonder why she's not picking out anything? She deserves to be dripped in silk and diamonds, anything she wants.

"Yes. Everything she touches, put it on my card." I hand over my platinum card without looking, only nodding my head towards Tillie so the employer knows who I mean.

"Sir...that's a lot of money," the annoying employee replies in a snooty voice and that's when I look down at her to see her shooting daggers at my queen with jealousy.

"You're right. Not only what she touches but looks at too. I would suggest you get started or I can find someone else to do it?" I threaten, watching her shake her head real fast and plaster on a fake smile as she races away to start loading her arms up with everything Tillie has touched so far.

Nicola is gesturing wildly and smacking Tillie, shoving something in her arms while dragging her to the dressing rooms. Well...This looks like an opportunity I can't pass up.

With a smirk, I slip past Nicola as she's distracted, mumbling to herself.

"Stubborn. Girls gotta feel sexy when down." A second later she flings a bra across the room and screams out loud while flushing with a dreamy sigh, "Dick! Good, big dick! Omg."

I bite my lip to not laugh as I pass her like a shadow, shaking my head as everyone stares at her which she chooses to ignore or doesn't care. I like this one, kid got balls. It seems like Nicola has some feelings for someone that's apparently on her mind if she's screaming in the store about some guy's dick.

Stepping into the dressing room, the only sound is the quiet rustling of clothes dropping to the floor. Each door is wide open but the one all the way in the back is closed shut. I head over there on silent feet and lean on the wall next to the door with my arms folded. My eyes slide shut at the sound of her clothes coming off her sexy body and her slow, even breathing like she's right next to me instead of being separated by a fucking door.

"Damn it. Why did I let her talk me into this? It feels like heaven against my skin," Tillie mutters to herself with a quiet drawn out moan.

What man can resist that one sound out of her pretty mouth? It's like an itch under your skin you can't reach but you can feel it all the same. I need to see her, to know what made that breathless moan escape past her lips. At this point, I don't care if I'm caught stalking her. At least she'll know I'm watching, maybe even feel me without seeing me. I like that thought. The way the small hairs on your nape rise because you know someone is staring. How your eyes dart in every direction to find the source and your heart starts racing. That gives me a thrill and knowing she's going to experience that when I'm watching her from the shadows...That alone gets my cock harder than anything else.

I'm a creep, sue me.

With a smirk, I test the door handle while debating how I'm going to sneak in behind her and instantly my lips twitch down into a deep frown.

Why the fuck didn't she lock the door?

To say I'm furious is an understatement. It's like she has no care for her safety. I mean, this makes it easier for me but it could have been anyone else trapping her in the back of the dressing room. No one would know. Anyone could come in here, look at her body, breathe on her smooth skin and take what's mine.

My eyes narrow as I slowly push the door open with the tip of my shoe as I lean against the opening of the door like I don't have a care in the world. But every muscle in my body is tight, bulging with how fucking mad I am.

Some of that anger dissolves into desire once I get a good look at her.

Like I said before, an angel in disguise to tempt a saint.

Beautiful.

A venus fly trap just waiting to capture her prey. A woman who knows what her body can do, how to use it to bring a man to his knees but chooses not to.

My eyes trail down her body, taking in the silk, white thong between her peach ass, and the straps that hold the garter belt up that's clenched around her waist and thighs. The little bow she plays with below her belly button is mesmerizing to watch, her slender fingers playing along the smooth texture. I grab my phone before I can think about it, snapping a photo of her. I have devious plans to send it to piss off some punks but I'm really taking it for myself.

A single word keeps running in circles in my head.

Mine.

Mine.

Fucking mine.

CHAPTER 6

Tillie

*D*o you know how hard it is to say no to someone like Nicola?

No?

Well, let me tell you... You can't.

It's like saying no to a Nun asking you to donate money to save the children. You're a freaking monster if you say no to the pleading eyes that hold some judgment if you slip anything less into her palm that isn't above a hundred bucks. Nicola is worse in person with getting what she wants, puppy eyes and pouting. She wasn't even in front of me as she demanded I sneak out of the compound and have a girls day with her. Just the sound of her pleading, she had me climbing a high fence before I was even off the phone with her.

The walls were closing in on me anyways so leaving was a no-brainer. I just had to sneak out without anyone seeing me and meet Nicola on the left side of the compound. All I needed was to steal one of Dalton's T-shirts and climb the fence. Easy but the barbed wire was not a pleasant experience. I used Dalton's shirt as a barrier and made it to the other side with only a few scrapes. The moment I hopped into Nicola's little, blue bug convertible, I was screaming at her to get us the hell out of there.

So, here we are. At the mall of all places where normal people hang out without a care in the world. Classical music, the mutter of excited shoppers, and once in a while, the screaming of an unhappy child that echoes from one side of the mall to the other. My body shudders each time it bounces off the walls, not being able to tell where the screams are coming from. Thank God I have Nicola on my side because each time she has a Tourettes episode, it eases something inside of me. Making me feel lighter and almost normal, a girls day of shopping with my friend. She laughs and skips, literally skips into stores, and doesn't give a damn about the stares. It makes me want to scream like a pterodactyl dinosaur at them just so they stop looking at her like there's something wrong with her.

She's my perfect friend and I'll cut a bitch who dares to hurt her innocent glow.

"So Evan and I did the dirty. I mean, there wasn't any..." She makes a gesture of her index finger going through her other finger which is shaped like a circle. "But I saw his penis which made me drool a bit but he didn't seem to mind. Apparently, spitting on a cock— Cock! is a turn-on. Who knew?" She shrugs her tiny shoulders but keeps making the crude gesture as if she can't stop.

People stare at Nicola each time she has a tick or yells something and I give them the middle finger as we walk past the idiots who have nothing better to do but judge others.

"Was this at the party last Saturday?" I ask absentmind-edly, shivering as I cross my arms over my breasts even though it's a pleasant, cool relief from the heat outside since we walked inside.

I feel like I have a target on the center of my back that says *look at me* and someone is moving in on me. I could just be paranoid, causing shivers to glide down my back with phantom hands. So much has happened in the last few days that inside I feel like a hollow shell. I should be rejoicing that Payne is finally dead, leaving me free to start living my life but I'm not. Something is missing. Maybe it's the many nights I stayed awake whilst images of Payne's death played out in my head. I was the one who always did the killing in them, making him suffer. His death was too simple, he got off easy instead of the drawn out pain I've been through for years.

It's like the universe is giving me the middle finger and having a laugh at my expense. There's still the fear of what now? Where do I go from here? I could just run, go somewhere that has a low population and no one would question where I'm from or why I'm there. Only problem with that is the guys. They wouldn't let me go, and the thing is... I don't see my life without them in it. They have caused me pain and humiliation but at the same time, they made me feel safe. Cared for under their cruel gazes. I think actions speak louder than words and to earn trust... They have to earn mine and I have to show that all I want from them is to be treated equally, and maybe one day down the road... loved without asking for anything in return.

"Was it obvious what we did? Nicky was not happy with me and I swear if lasers could shoot out of his eyes, Evan would have been on the receiving end." Nicola picks up a pink top, holds it up to me, and shakes her head while tossing it back on the clothing rack.

"You're fine. It looked like you were just kissing," I lie through my teeth, pretending to be occupied by some clothes on the next rack.

Her lipstick was smeared that night, and her hair a wild mess but I probably didn't look any better. My stomach heats and my thighs clench at the memory of Dalton pounding into me as I slipped Tey's beautiful cock into my mouth. After all the shit I've seen over the years, you would not think watching Nicky torturing the meathead jock would make me moan louder just so I could see him stab the fucker again.

"Yeah riiight. It looked like you were just kissing too but for the love of God, don't share the details. That's my brother." She makes a face like she ate something bad and shudders.

She shudders again and jerks a couple of items off the hangers, throwing them on the ground. After she's done, she sighs and bends down to pick them up while I help her.

"As long as Evan treats you right and it feels good... just go with those feelings." That's my advice and I'm sticking with it.

You don't always get to experience a first kiss, a first love, the first time two bodies come together as if made for each other. Sometimes that all gets taken from you.

"I forget that we've only been friends for a while, it feels like years. I'm not throwing away something that is good in my life." She doesn't look me in the eye as she turns and walks out of the store.

I follow until I'm caught up with her and stop her by the elbow outside a window full of mannequins with only underwear on.

"I'll do everything I can to help you, even making sure your pain in my ass brother doesn't interfere." I hold my pinky up towards her, and she flashes me a grin before hooking hers through mine.

"Thanks, Tillie. He's different around you, you know? Not as intense as our father." She instantly frowns and shakes her head like she's trying to get rid of a memory. "Let's go in here! It's just what we need!" She grabs my wrist, and drags me inside the underwear shop with an excited squeal, quickly letting go to start loading her arms with lingerie.

Goosebumps rise on my arms when I feel it. I swear someone is drilling a hole into the back of my head. Trying not to be obvious, I glance over my shoulder and look around to see if anyone is staring at me. I only find a group of ignorant guys shoving each other as they stare once they walk by but they're not who I'm looking for. This feeling is intense, hot on my body like they're taking their time watching my every move.

"Tillie! We both need something sexy, it boosts confidence and it will drive the guys crazy. I wonder what Evan would like? I don't see any Star Wars underwear but they have Wonder Woman!" Nicola races towards the back of the store as I trail behind, feeling out of my element.

I never got to pick out my underwear in a place like this. It usually was a sexy shop with costumes and the skimpiest lingerie for working the poles at night. It was only to be worn so greens would fall on the stage under the loud music and when my legs were wrapped around the cold, slippery steel of the pole stripping. The rest of my underwear was Goodwill, the thought alone makes me shudder. I can't help skimming my fingers across the soft textures, the ones that feel like air between my fingers. A woman wears panties like this, a matching set to feel like she can take on the world.

I blow out a breath, feeling my chest tighten, and finally catch up with Nicola. She shoves something in my arms before I can blink and pushes me towards the dressing rooms.

I'm not sure why but everything lately to me feels unreal, like I'm constantly walking in a daze. Honestly, I don't know why I picked the last door on the end, maybe because I feel safer all the way back where hiding is easier? One second I'm standing in front of a full-length mirror fully dressed and the next I'm slipping on the smooth material of lingerie. Everything I do feels almost robotic, I'm not even sure what's happening to me. Have I finally broken down? Am I damaged beyond repair? Has it come to this?

I usually avoid looking in a mirror, I mean *really* looking at my reflection as if you're staring at someone else, examining every single imperfection right down to your very soul. I can recognize the scars because it's become part of me that tells a story of what I've been through. The tattoos speak of control over myself, hiding the pain from the outside world. But for the life of me, I don't recognize my face. It's not the features I've always despised inheriting, it was thinking Payne was part of me. I have Diana's eyes, right down to how expressive they are, but who else do I see on my face if not him? Where do my full lips come from? The shape of my chin?

Fiddling with the bow that slips through my fingers like water, I try not to think of what happened at Logan's house. Seeing the rage in Diana's eyes, it was downright hateful. She probably never wants to see me again. I'm not even going to start thinking of what Franco did, I just can't right now. It's all too much. I can't really blame Diana if she forbids me from seeing her but I have something inside of me eating away. I need to know who my father is. It's almost noticeable now that Payne isn't shown in my features, he never was a father figure, and seeing how nothing on my face looks like him makes it seem as if I've never really looked at myself.

"Hey, mama." That raspy, smooth voice makes it feel like hot, scalding water is sliding down my spine, enough to make me shiver from the heat but wanting to burn my flesh away just to feel warm.

I lift my head and my gaze connects with his dark ones that are reminiscent of a black abyss. You can't look away even if you tried, you want to tip forward and see where it takes you.

"Dom." I pry my eyes away with a great deal of difficulty, not in the least bit ashamed of how much skin I'm showing in front of him.

His gaze feels familiar on my back, hot and intense. I'm not surprised by this at all. I should have figured it out.

"You've been following me?" I question, not looking up as I continue playing with the silk bow.

My breath leaves me in a sharp gasp as rough, big hands grasp my shoulders and spin me around before walking me backwards until my back collides with the mirror. The cold glass on my back makes me shiver but my front is warm, really warm from Dom crowding my space with his whole, tall, muscled body.

"It's like you're asking me to throw you over my shoulder and keep you for myself." His minty breath washes over my face as he comes closer until the tip of his nose is barely skimming mine. "You're lucky it's only me stalking you. You've been very naughty, mama. Why did you sneak out?" he asks, bringing his big hand up to cup my cheek like I'm made of fragile glass.

He's staring at me like I am unbreakable, strong with those dark eyes of his but we both know that just the slightest pressure of his hand could break me into pieces. I bet he could end everything without breaking a sweat and I wonder how many people he's killed with his scarred hands. Yeah, I noticed that right away at the rave. They're the hands of a fighter, cut open many times and healed but only to reopen again. It's such a weird feeling, he's purposely holding back and being gentle with me. Some people can spend forever together and still feel like they are just finding out new things about their loved one but looking into Dom's eyes doesn't feel that way. I've only met him once and I felt safe, comfortable in my own skin. This is our second time meeting but it feels like we've been doing this for centuries. Familiar and easy, like gravity pulling you tight together because you're meant to be near each other.

"I needed to get out. I couldn't breathe." The words fall out of my mouth truthfully and easily.

"I should kill those punks, but I have a feeling you wouldn't be too pleased with me if I did." His thumb glides from the corner of my bottom lip slowly to the other side, making my mouth part at the feeling washing over me.

Rough and warm.

"I–I don't want that. It's not about them. You should stay away from me. Everyone who comes near me ends up getting hurt." I swallow thickly as I look up at him from under my lashes, wanting to take back my words and knowing I can't because it's true.

Everyone I care about gets hurt because of me.

Dom leans his upper body away, trapping my lower half to the mirror with his as he stares down at me with an angry expression. So passionate with his dark eyes, narrow, thick brows, and thick lips that tighten with his emotions. He moves his rock-hard thigh between my legs and takes my face between both of his palms so I'm fully looking up at him.

"If I ever hear those words out of this perfect mouth again, I'll fuck you until the only word you know is my name. I'll drag out so many orgasms from you and keep going, even when you're begging me to stop. I'd do it right now, but it seems luck is on your side today. I imagine they'll be here any minute so me being right here in front of you should tell you that I'm not going anywhere. A King never leaves his Queen behind."

I don't grasp what he's saying about someone coming soon because all my attention is on the promise he makes that heats every part of my body like it's on fire. My pussy clenches, empty and dripping wet with my new panties sticking to my lower lips. His harsh, thick lips curl into a smirk as he stares into my eyes as if he knows how my body is reacting to him.

I don't even have time to argue or sass back to prove he's wrong even though he's not. He pushes me further into the mirror, and my body arches as his thigh rises higher between my legs until he's rubbing right against my clit. My body shudders, hips rolling to seek more pleasure as I rub my hands up and down his muscular chest. I imagine I'm soaking his pants, that he can feel my juices smearing all over him. I don't have time to feel embarrassed about it though, I just keep rocking my hips against his muscular thighs and bite back a whimper as he rubs perfectly in the right spot on my clit. Every sound that escapes my mouth is loud and echoes in the dressing room. My body slows slightly, only realizing where the hell I am but Dom puts a stop to that right away. His calloused hand grabs the back of my neck and tilts my head by placing his thumb on my jaw to angle how he wants me. The first brush of his lips is soft, warm, and light like he's teasing me but cherishing me at the same time. I moan without caring who hears, parting my mouth to push my lips harder against his until he fucking destroys me.

Devours me.

Like I'm his last meal and he plans on savoring me.

He groans deep in his throat, tightening his fingers around the back of my neck, and slides his tongue along my bottom lip. I grip at his taped waist, grabbing fistfuls of his shirt as I ride his thigh faster and tilt my head back more as I try to get impossibly closer to him.

He rips his mouth away, breathing hard as he places his other hand on the mirror like he needs to support himself and rests his forehead against mine. His long fingers massage the back of my neck, tightening and loosening as if he's trying to hold himself back. I like that, he needs to contain his need around me and let me ride out my pleasure.

"That's it, mama. Ride my thigh. Push that gorgeous pussy harder against me and soak my jeans until I have a wet spot on my thigh from all those juices dripping out just for me. Come for Papi." He holds my gaze, tightening his grip on my neck when my eyes start to close as pleasure washes over me.

I don't hold back my moans, not caring if anyone hears. My breath comes out in hard pants as I stare at him, the way my body shakes and clenches tells me he's going to have a very obvious wet spot on his thigh. I feel like liquid, boneless, and finally feel like my chest isn't as tight as before.

"There she is, my Queen." He places a tender kiss on my forehead, staying for a second longer before reluctantly stepping away. "I have to go. Be a good girl, mama. I'll be watching." My stalker winks and turns towards the open door but before he disappears I blurt the words out of my mouth.

"Why do you call me mama?"

He glances over his shoulder and smiles devilishly at me like he knows something I don't.

"What else would I call the future mother of my children?" he says before leaving while I stand there like a fish out of water.

Did that just happen? He came in like a devil in disguise, all quiet and mysterious, gave me pleasure without asking anything in return and kissed me like I'm his. And he left just as he came, like a dream... as if he was never really here. The throbbing between my legs and the panties I now have to buy because of the very noticeable wet spot in the front are the only evidence he was here.

Oh shit.

I clasp back against the mirror as my legs shake like jello and stare at nothing. With a groan, I lean over to grab my jeans off the chair in the corner and turn towards the mirror again.

It's the outline of my ass print on the glass that has the first giggle coming out of my mouth. Then it's my flush cheeks and the bird's nest in my hair all while standing in my underwear in the dressing room that makes me smile at my reflection. I just came in a very public place that has walls that bounce off sounds, making everything louder.

Blowing out an exhausted but oddly relaxed breath, I start to put my jeans on and that's how I'm caught. With my pants around my ankles and bent over, I look up to find a very pissed off Logan in the doorway as he pants for breath like he just ran a marathon. I really should learn how to lock a door.

"You have five seconds to get your ass dressed or I'm carrying you out of here just as you are," he grinds out between his teeth and roams his gaze down my body, pausing at the space between my thighs.

His eyes narrow into slits and I swear his nostrils flare like an angry bull. Yup, I'm caught red-handed, there's absolutely no way of hiding what went on in here. Now I understand what Dom meant. He ratted me out.

He has some balls, I'll give him that. Last time we all met, Logan and Dom looked like they wanted to go at each other's throats. This must be his way of taunting his enemy.

"Stop staring at me like that and don't fucking tell me what to do," I reply back just as angrily, pulling my pants up the rest of the way and shoving my shirt over my head in jerky movements.

"I'll stare if I want to. You're mine, baby girl. My property and nobody touches what's mine without my fucking permission. And I'll tell you what to do— Where are you going?!" He's shouting now as I shove past him and practically stomp out of the dressing room with him hot on my heels.

"Away from you!" I shout right back at him, meeting eyes with Nicola who's standing next to her brother near the store entrance with a look of pity on her face.

Great. Just great. The whole gang's here.

I quicken my steps, beyond pissed off. I'm so furious at all of them I can't even look into their eyes. I'm trying to make my great escape without having to deal with them when the saleslady stops right in front of me with arms full of shopping bags.

"Excuse me, miss. Don't forget your purchases." She quickly starts shoving the bags after bags in my hands that hold expensive lingerie judging by the price tags I've seen.

"What? No. I didn't buy these." I try handing them back but she steps away with a tight smile and nervously glances over my shoulder before looking away.

"They are already paid for. Have a nice day," she mutters fast and dodges around me like I'm going to bite her or something.

I take a peek in the bags and realize it's everything I was admiring while walking around the store. Dom. His stalking skills are kind of impressive but I really didn't need all of this even though it's sweet of him to do it in a weird, but extremely hot way.

With a huff, I try to stride past Nicky without looking at him but I look out of the corner of my eye because I can't help myself. He's already staring at me, raising one single brow, and glances from my bags then back to my eyes with a knowing look. He doesn't look happy as he drags Nicola by her arm out of the store ahead of Logan and I without a word to me.

"Are those from *him*?" Logan growls behind me. I can almost hear his teeth gashing together.

He has no right to be angry about this. I didn't ask Dom to buy me anything. I didn't ask for anything that's been happening to me since I was born. I really want to turn around and yell at him, punch him. Let him feel my pain by giving him some. But I don't. After what happened in his house, it's hard to even look at him. I don't want to see the disgust on his handsome face or loathing. I just can't handle it, not when I'm this weak.

I don't bother replying. I just quicken my pace which, of course, his long legs match until he's walking right next to me with his hands in his pants pockets. He's quiet, only exhaling a long sigh every few minutes like he wants to say something but doesn't. I can hear Nicky speaking quietly to Nicola as he bends his head closer to hers and opens the door for her that leads outside.

"It was reckless and stupid. You both could have been hurt. Do you have any idea what it would do to me if you or her got hurt? Stop taking these chances, Nicola, especially right now," he whispers to her, talking in a soothing tone.

My heart does a small skip in my chest and my throat closes at how gentle he's being with her. Nicky is always so reserved, his features are void of emotions but you can tell he really does care for his sister and he added me to that too.

The California sun is blinding when I step out after them and squint against the light while shielding my face with my hand. I almost run back inside when I see the entrance lined up with bikers, their motorcycles familiar and loudly deafening. That sound rumbles into my chest and scares me for a split second until my gaze lands on Dalton sitting on his bike in the front of the line of bikers. For one second, I thought it was Payne. I thought he was here for me but he's dead.

He's dead. He can't hurt you anymore.

"Little Bitch! You. Are. In. Trouble." For some reason, I can hear every word Dalton says over the rumble of engines and oh man he's pissed. His violet eyes are like a storm rolling in, not the usually light purple I've come to love gazing into.

Even though I've been at the club for a couple of days, I haven't met anyone since I was confined to Dalton's room. I was okay with that but those walls seemed to get smaller and smaller each day. I won't be locked up again, I can't. I don't know what that will do to my mental health. Maybe the next time will send me over the edge but I'm not willing to test it. He'll have to understand. I wasn't running from them. I just needed a little normal in my life. To pretend everything is okay.

"I got her, Dalt. We'll meet you back at your club, brother. Nicky, let Tey know after he's done with his errand that it's time we all had a chat." Logan shoots off commands like a pissed off drill sergeant, crowding against my back and nudging me forward without waiting for a reply from the guys.

With his hand on the small of my back, Logan guides me past the line of bikers that rumble out of the parking lot with a hand signal from Dalton. I pause in front of Nicola with an eye roll and ignore her brother as he glares at me.

"You mind holding on to these for me?" I gesture to the bags hanging off my arms and hold out my hands.

"Yeah. Don't worry. They will be in safe hands— Hey! Nicolas!" Nicola shouts at her brother who grabs the bags out of my hands with another glare thrown my way and walks off without saying anything.

Rude.

Nicola shakes her head and starts yelling in Japanese as she runs to catch up with him. They climb into his Nissan and peel out of the parking lot.

Logan's hand slips down my spine, right above my ass as he guides me to keep moving and off to the right on the sidewalk until a gleaming, pitch-black crotch rocket comes into view.

I admittedly stop in front of his bike and cross my arms with a stubborn jerk of my chin. Although I'd like nothing better than to hop on this badass crotch rocket and take off, zooming past traffic at dangerous levels, that's not happening because the owner of the bike is a jackass.

"I'm not getting on that with you," I say as I glare up at

him, feeling my stomach drop as his honey colored eyes meet mine with that same challenging glare.

"Yes, you are." He towers over me, blocking out the sunlight in my eyes and letting me see the dark challenge in his beautiful eyes.

I tilt my head towards the sky, exhaling a long breath in defeat. He'd probably throw me over the seat and strap me down, not caring one bit if anyone sees him manhandling me.

One of these days... we are going to come to a head and combust without warning, I just hope it doesn't destroy us in the end.

"Fine," I mutter and shove him aside to swing my leg over, scooting back to make room for him in front.

"You didn't have a choice anyways." He just has to get the last word in.

I'm going to murder him but I might use that big dick energy he has one last time as a hooray for old-time sakes.

CHAPTER 7

Logan

She's squeezing me so tight that one would think she's purposely trying to cut off my air supply by crushing my lungs. Tillie's been silent and stiff for half the ride as we weave through downtown traffic but her fingers that grip around my ribs move every so often in small caresses. She can scream and deny it but she's attracted to me just as much as I am to her. I won't admit that to her. She could use that against me, she really doesn't know the power she already has over me.

She suddenly smacks my back and squeezes me tighter with her other hand as I drive along the coast. One side of the street is store after store and restaurants, while across the street are miles and miles of sandy beaches. I pull into a parking lot with not many cars and stop my bike, the engine vibrating under us until I shut that off too. The only sound is seagulls, the crash of waves, and barking way down the beach shore. Before I can get off my bike, Tillie is swinging off and kicking off her shoes without pausing as she rushes through the sand towards the ocean. My laugh isn't quiet as I follow behind her, amused at her child-like wonder as she runs into the salty water. She kicks up water and stops at knee level, bending down slightly to run her fingers along the surface of the ocean. I left my shoes near my bike and I'm not going to bother rolling up my pants as I follow after her until the water is gently splashing around my calves.

"I've never seen the ocean. It stretches so far... you really could wander out there and never return," she whispers eerily, shaking her head and crossing her arms over her stomach like she is cold.

The sun will be setting soon, within another hour. The water lapping at our legs is warm so I know she's not cold. Her mind must be somewhere else and that bugs me to no end. I never know what's going on in that beautiful head of hers, and I want to. I want to know *everything* about her. What she thinks about, dreams about...

"Why did you leave the compound? Do you not know the risks you took today?" I question, staring at her side profile when she refuses to meet my gaze.

"Risks? My life is one big risk. I won't be locked away again. I may not look like it but I'm not completely fragile. I refuse to be treated like a damsel in distress. Get that through your big head." She finally glances up at me, her lips in a frown, and a wrinkle between her brows.

I don't like seeing that look on her face. She always has her shoulders straight like everyone else is beneath her and head held high even when she's thrust into dangerous situations that would make anyone else crumble. It's one of the reasons I admire her.

"I've never thought of you as weak, baby girl. We have enemies all around us, waiting for one slip up. You could have been kidnapped in broad daylight and raped, tortured. Don't you know what we would do if you were taken from us? This city would be torn apart. You should have asked one of us to go with you if you needed to leave for a while." I clear my throat, hating how raspy my voice is, she fucking scared me today. Anything could have happened to her and I wouldn't have been by her side to keep her safe.

She stares up at me in surprise as she turns fully towards me and tilts her head in puzzlement.

"Ask one of you? Dalton got hurt because of me and everything at the club, all the responsibilities he has now... I can't ask him to do that for me. I haven't seen the rest of you guys for days and I can't really blame you for not wanting me around. I–I feel disgusted with myself." She swallows thickly and gazes off to the side, watching the sun dipping down slowly across the horizon.

I place my finger under her chin and make her look at me.

"What the hell are you talking about? What happened wasn't your fault. There's always going to be a bad guy out there that wants to come after us. That's why I'm trying to keep you safe and you keep making that difficult." I stroke her cheekbone, wondering how she's crept into my heart so suddenly and unexpectedly.

"Everything is my fault and that's why I'm leaving, Lo. Everyone who I start to care for gets hurt or worse." She bites her lip and takes a step away from me, turning away to start heading back towards the shore.

I grip her elbow and tug her towards me until she's plastered to my front, her fingers spread over my chest to keep her balance. She looks up at me with her lips parted and a flash of anger crosses her face when I don't let go of her as she pushes against me.

"You aren't going anywhere, baby girl. That day when I said you're mine, I meant what I said. Mine to hurt. Mine to kiss. Mine to fuck. Mine to protect. You can shout it to the rooftops until your throat is sore but we both know that you want to be right by my side." I tighten my grip on her as she struggles in my hold, her fists slamming against me over and over.

I grab her wrists, putting the slightest pressure on her skin until she goes lax in my grip. My hands lace with her delicate fingers as I drag her hands up my chest and behind my neck until she's holding on to me. Placing my index finger back under her chin, I lean down as she stands on her toes to reach me. It's the softest touch of our lips, her mouth plump and like silk as I glide mine back and forth over hers. I don't rush our first kiss. It's painfully slow and heated, our mouths hardly touching like we're afraid we might burn with the slightest movement. Her fingernails dig into the back of my neck as if she's holding back as we breathe each other in. Sharing oxygen. She's the sun and moon, combined together right as they are passing each other across time and space. She can burn me by just looking at me and she's as luminous as the moon that she lights up my nights.

When the fuck did I become a romantic? What is she doing to me? Next thing I know I'll be outside her window with a boombox playing a lovesick song. At least that's better than spilling Romeo shit like Juliet, let down your hair so I can climb into your window and sex you up. I might be getting my stories mixed up but each has the same ending. Some guy climbing through her window to fuck.

My nose runs along one side of hers, inhaling deep as I place another light as a feather kiss on her perfect lips. I lean back and notice her eyes are closed, her face still tilted towards me.

"Why are you staring at me? I can feel it. I don't know how you stand to look at me after what hap–happened with Franco." Her bottom lip trembles but she keeps her eyes closed.

I'm glad her eyes are closed, she can't see the flash of anger that passes over my face. But it's not because of her. It's all for my father. My fucking father. I can't trust him, I don't think I have for a long time. He's not who he used to be. The phrase in our family always was blood is thicker than water but his blood is looking pretty mucky these days. He's going to pay for what he did to Tillie. He touched my property. It pissed me off more than Dom did. For some reason, I don't have the urge to kill him, maybe spill a little blood but nothing compares to what I want to do to Franco.

I do want to kill my father.

"Look at me," I demand, grabbing her chin as she squeezes her eyes shut and whimpers when my touch becomes painful.

Wide, chocolate brown eyes gaze up at me with unshed tears

"It's not your fault. It's his. He could have stopped it, Tillie but he decided to play into Payne's sick game. Franco has a motive for everything and he wants your fear. He can control you that way... don't give it to him okay?" I'm speaking from experience, I have the scars from his belt on my back to prove it even though most have faded over time.

"Dad?" I walked into his office, his head bent over the desk as he looked over papers and a glass of dark liquid that smelled strong in his hand.

I wasn't allowed in his office when the door was shut or when he had guests over. The one man in dark suits and scary, cruel slanted eyes always came over. Ever since Mother passed away, he's been in my dad's office almost every day.

I don't like him. He stared at me with a face that could have been made from stone but his dark green eyes made me scared to enter my dad's office. He's a bad man, I wasn't sure how I could tell. It could be the quiet way he sat on the couch, observing everything with calculating eyes. He's the kind of man you ran from if you happened to bump into him on the street.

"*What do you need, Logan?*" *Dad looked angry at me for interrupting but I couldn't get rid of the lady at the front door.*

"*There's a lady in the living room wanting to talk about Mom. She said she works for, uh, the times?*" *I tried to remember what she said but it's hard to pay attention to anything.*

I miss my mom. She's all I could think about. It's been six months, but it felt like just yesterday that she was murdered.

"*I'll get rid of her.*" *The man stood from the couch and buttoned his suit jacket as he walked to the door but he paused in the doorway to look back at my dad. "I would suggest teaching him now while he's young, Franco. Discipline makes them loyal and stronger.*" *With that being said, he walked out the door and shut it behind him.*

I stood there before my dad's desk, watched as he tossed his drink back, and slammed it on the table after he finished it. He looked at me for a while, his expression almost sad before he hardened his features. His lips tightened at the edges before his gaze narrowed on me with a look I never had seen on him before. He always used to laugh but that went away just like my mom. He stood and walked around his desk while unbuckling his belt and snapping it from the loops as he stopped right in front of me.

I wanted to back away, but instead eyed him warily because he was scaring me. Why did he look like my dad but didn't at the same time?

"*Things are changing, Logan. Jin is right. I've been letting you get away with a lot lately but it's time you learn that you can't stay a child forever. It's time to grow up. Turn around and take off your shirt. You won't move or make a sound. Is that understood?*" *His words were harsh and low, meaning he meant every word with his voice deep with authority.*

I didn't see any other choice. My dad was all I had left and he needed me. I silently took my shirt off and presented my back while my whole body shook in fear.

This was my chance to prove that I'm not a kid anymore, life taught me if you're soft even at a young age... those around you die. You can't protect them if you're not a grown man.

"This is just the beginning, son. We are all going to make them pay, but first, we have to toughen you up for this new life of ours. First rule. Don't ever talk to reporters," Dad said with a hand on my shoulder then he stepped away with a squeeze.

It was silent until I heard a sharp sound through the air and a loud crack. Then there was blistering, hot pain across my back. My body jerked forward, and I caught myself with my hands on the edge of the desk and heaved for breath from the agony.

"Again. Sit up straight," my dad said in a hard, empty voice.

I shook my head and gritted my teeth as I sat up again. The second hit was worse than the first. It felt like my back was set on fire. I bit my lip so hard as I held in a scream that blood filled my mouth. It went on and on that eventually, the strikes along my skin went numb. My back was so straight that when Dad dropped his belt on the floor, my shoulders hunched forward as silent tears ran down my cheeks.

"First rule, Logan?" he questioned from behind me, his hand once again laying on my shoulder.

"Don't talk to reporters, Franco," I rasped out, breathing hard and wincing when he squeezed my shoulder before leaving his office without another word.

I collapsed against the wood floor, gasping through the pain.

I also realized something very important. We are never going back to how things used to be and my dad wasn't Dad anymore.

He was Franco.

I shake myself out of the memory, feeling like my back is burning with the old memories. Franco stopped beating me with his belt once I learned that I was strong enough to stop him the older I got. That's when I became a man in his eyes and he started trusting me to take over some of the business side of things. Like killing a man at age twelve.

Tillie's been gazing up at me for a long time in silence as I was lost in thought. Her eyes are so expressive that she wears her emotions on her sleeves. Pain, fear, and lastly, determination.

"Okay." She nods her head slowly and her shoulders relax gradually. "But, Logan... you can't hurt me again. I need you to prove to me that you won't turn cruel the moment it strikes you. No more. I can handle some pain physically, and to be honest, I enjoy that part of you but emotionally I can't do tha–that. No secrets or lies. Promise me." She has a desperate tone in her voice, like the smallest movement and wrong answer from me will break her.

I'm going to show her how strong she is. She can take anything thrown her way. That's why she's one of us, meant to be.

"I promise. No more secrets." I hope I can keep that promise to her but if her life is in danger I might need to break it.

She leans her forehead on my bicep with a deep breath as I stroke my fingers through her long hair. The purple is really fading from her hair, the dark brown showing more.

"I need the same from you too though, baby girl. No secrets. We need to know everything." I hate even saying that but if she keeps it to herself, it's a barrier between us and an obstacle to actually keeping her safe.

I just hope she doesn't hear about what I've been up to since she's been staying at Dalton's. She won't trust me ever again. Last time she saw me with Paris, she sent me a look of loathing like she couldn't stand the sight of me. I'm trying here, but I'm not perfect and never will be. Everything I do is to keep her safe and if that means hurting her in the process, so be it.

"Not today. Just not today okay? Soon." She stiffens in my arms and steps back with a sad smile.

"Very soon. We can't wait long. I'll let the guys know you

need more time." She nods and grabs my hand as she starts walking back towards the shore just as the sun starts to disappear along the water's edge.

She suddenly stops in the middle of the beach and turns towards me with a worried expression.

"What di–did you guys do with Pay–Payne's body and the rest of the Demon Jokers?" She stumbles over her words and does that thing again where her eyes go distant like she's somewhere else.

"You don't have to worry about him ever again. He's gone for good. We sent his head back in a box to the rest of the Demon Jokers along with the rest of them scattered in hazard containers. Don't worry about him anymore," I reassure her and guide her back to my bike with her hand wrapped in mine as she trails behind me.

"That's not who I'm worried about," she mutters under her breath so quietly to herself I almost don't hear her.

We need to have that talk sooner rather than later.

"Come on. Let's get you back to Dalton. He's probably going out of his mind." I stop by my bike and watch her easily climb on like she's done it a million times.

She grasps my palm and swings her leg over the seat while making room for me. Once I'm in front of her, her arms immediately circle my waist and hold on tight.

"Logan?" she whispers in my ear from behind, lips grazing my earlobe.

"Yeah?" I say over my shoulder, feeling her cheek rest along mine.

"You're still an asshole. Don't betray me, or you'll wish you never did," she threatens darkly and in a low, seductive whisper.

Son of a bitch. Every single time. She only has to breathe or look at me and I instantly want her.

"I'll probably always be an asshole, baby girl. Trust me," I reply back and start my bike with a twist of my wrist, drowning out any response she would have.

Fuck. I'm screwed.

CHAPTER 8

Cruz

'*ve always found it fascinating when someone is on the brink of death how much they beg, willing to give anything up to me just to see another sunrise. It's pathetic really. They don't deserve to live and it will be my hand to bring them to their end as it should be.

"Are you done playing with your toys, Cruz, or can we move on?" Nix questions me from his spot by the door he's been leaning against since we arrived.

I found this abandoned factory and set it up as a shop of horrors for a few days. Screams really echo in here, bouncing back to me like a never-ending loop of torture. Makes my dick hard.

I don't respond back to Nix. The fuckhead's been getting on my nerves for days. Checking in with Payne and reporting everything I'm doing like some babysitter. I should just kill him. Tempting, very tempting but not just yet.

Nix rolls his eyes and fishes out his phone when it starts to ring, strolling to the other side of the building out of earshot. I turn back towards the mess in front of me and can't stop the smile spreading across my lips at the sight. Slicking back my dirty blond hair, I walk around the area from all sides, feeling nothing and everything at the same time.

When I first grabbed the trucker outside of the hotel, I kept him alive for a couple of days until I had all the information I needed. It was easy pulling out answers to the questions I had for him, but the way he squealed like a pig as I peeled off layers of his skin until he was just a meat bag? The animalistic sounds still ring in my ears, making my endorphins high for days.

He begged for mercy but I wasn't feeling very happy with him. By his answers, he didn't seem to know much about the girl he picked up in the middle of the desert. But I could smell a lie, he was trying to be brave by not giving up Tillie. I was growing bored and when I'm bored, the real fun begins. He started singing eventually but what he gave me only pissed me the fuck off. He got to the part of her giving him a lap dance and never seeing her again, and that's when I saw red, knowing he touched what's mine. I pulled more information out of him by slowly torturing him. He told me everything by the time I was pulling his toenails off with my knife digging under his nails. He dropped her off at the bus station downtown and if he took too long to answer every single detail, I started prying out his teeth by cutting his gums with my knife.

So here we are days later, trucker Adam dead in the corner of the room and my next victim ready for a torture session. An old, abandoned tire factory is the perfect place to hear the young employee who works at the bus station sobbing for her life. Everything echoes right back to me.

"Please. I don't know anything. She bought two different bus tickets but I'm not sure which one she got on! That's all I know!" she cried out, her gaze trying to follow me as I circled her.

Once the truck driver, Adam, told me he dropped Tillie off at the bus station, I didn't waste any time. Okay, I took my time killing him but the moment I was done, I was striding into the bus station. You know, I don't always have to torture someone to get what I want. I can be charming too to get what I need from people. That didn't work with the annoying fucking bitch working at the bus station though. When I showed Tillie's picture and asked if she'd seen her, the response I got was a shrug and her popping her bubblegum in my face. Knocking her out cold with the butt of my gun and kidnapping her was almost too easy at the end of her night shift. I enjoyed watching the confusion in her eyes when she finally woke up, finding her body trapped and the smell of death and tar had her screaming within seconds. It hasn't even been an hour and she's already telling me everything so she can live. I never said I wouldn't kill her, she just assumed I'd set her free.

"And where did she go?" I ask from behind her, bending down to grab the gasoline tank at my feet and pulling my lighter out of my pocket.

"I told you already. Her tickets were for New York and California. Please. Let me go!" She struggled in her awkward position, trying to get out of the tires that I had stacked from her feet to shoulders.

"You didn't have to end up here in this situation but you know what I hate most?" I ask her, ignoring her whimpers and starting to splash gasoline on her. "People who think I owe them something. I owe no one anything! I'm above you all and that's why you're going to die. Should have answered my questions the first time instead of being a cunt and you might have lived."

She screams and calls for help but no one will be coming to her rescue. It would be too late anyways. I flip open the lighter and smile as I throw it at her. The flames instantly light the tires on fire surrounding her and her shrieks get louder as her flesh sizzles and pops. It starts to smell like burnt meat but I don't care. I'm here to watch the show as her skin melts off until bone peaks through. Eventually, she stops screaming as she slowly dies but the tires keep her body burning until only what will remain of her will be burnt flesh stuck to the tires.

"Cruz!" Nix calls out from somewhere behind me, keeping a distance, but I don't bother looking at him when I have a show in front of me for my entertainment.

"What?" I scowl at the remaining flames, annoyed that he's interrupting my *me* time.

"Something happened. We need to get to the club. Right now."

The first thought I had upon arriving back at the club for the first time in two months is that it's going to be some stupid bullshit. Missing drugs or some shit, which tends to happen when you have a bunch of bikers that are hooked to the shit. But I didn't think I'd be opening a perfectly wrapped package with a fucking head inside. I wasn't sure what the big deal was at first. Just someone out there missing a body part, but once I pulled the head out and held it up to the rest of the Demon Jokers surrounding me, I realized what a prize I had in my hand. My fist gripped handfuls of hair as Payne's head dangled in the air, his expression one of surprise. The bastard thought he was invincible, it's almost a shame I didn't get to kill him myself. This makes it easier to take Tillie without having to get this fucker's permission to have her to myself. Not like that would stop me anyways.

"Any idea who did this?" I ask the men around me, noticing some missing members like Poe and Whiskey until I see some more packages scattered on the bar top.

Is that a foot sticking out of the top of the box? I have to admit, I'm impressed. No postage or any hints of where their bodies were chopped up at or where they came from. I'll find out eventually. Nothing gets by me. I'm smarter than all the mindless, boring people.

"Not yet but it's only a matter of time. This means war. Whoever did this came after our club and president," someone mutters, my eyes connecting to the prospect whose name I don't bother remembering.

Just another body that's breathing in his meat suit before he dies.

"I want answers now. What has Payne been up to in my absence?" I ask out loud, meeting anyone's gaze who has the balls to meet my eyes.

When no one says anything, I raise a brow and slam Payne's head down on the table. As I let go, a streak of shredded skin and muscles smear across the surface of the wood as his head rolls off and topples to the dirty floor.

"I'm your president now. Being Vice makes me next in line. I want some fucking answers. Now!" Cracking my neck, I plaster on a fake ass smile that strains my lips and gaze each member in the eye as I pretend to be anything but angry. "Okay, who is going to tell me what I missed while I was gone?" I calmly ask and feel smug when these lowlifes don't question me being Prez.

They could have a vote but then I'd have to start killing them off one at a time for voting against me and I'm pretty sure they know this.

"Payne was on a bender again. Keeping his whereabouts mainly to himself and took his most trusted club members with him. All we know is he was visiting another motorcycle club somewhere in California." The prospect speaks up again and it's as if the kid thinks he can impress me by squaring his shoulders while looking me in the eye.

It doesn't work but he has more balls than most of these fuckers avoiding my gaze. He does have my attention though when most would bore me. I'm eager to hear what he knows about California.

"What's your name one-percenter?" I walk towards him, enjoying the fear that flashes in his eyes for a split-second before he clears his throat as I stop in front of him.

"Taz," he mutters and gets shifty-eyed as I place my hand on his shoulder and steer him towards my new office, Payne's old office.

"You're dismissed!" I say loudly enough for everyone to hear me, the sound of stomping boots quickly leaving the room hardens my smile. One command and they go running like the devil is chasing after them. Nix shakes his head and walks out slowly, he better fall in line. I don't care if he hates me or how I'm going to run this club. If I say jump, he better ask how high. Everyone will obey me.

Useless cowards.

I turn my attention back to Taz and my smile slips off my face when I shut the door behind us, rounding the desk. Taking a seat, I prop my feet on the desk surface and stare at Taz for a long time as he fidgets near the door.

"I see a promotion in your future very soon, Taz. Tell me everything you've heard. California you said?"

I shiver in delight. It looks like we will be taking a visit out to California. I just need to figure out which club Payne went to. I can feel it. Mine. My little bird is hiding in the sunny state and I can't wait to find her.

"I might be able to help. I've heard some things whenever Payne was high. He had some ties with a gang out there on the west side. Muerte or something like that." Lorrie's smoker voice speaks up as she pushes through the door without knocking, letting me know she was eavesdropping, and plants her skinny ass on my lap.

Her eyes are glazed, blown wide from cocaine or whatever shit she's on these days. I hide my disgust with a stoic expression, leaning back in my chair as I stare at her weathered face from years of drug abuse.

"Since when?" I wave my hand at Taz, dismissing him as I rub my blond beard with my other hand.

"Since they started supplying hardcore drugs to our club and offering a lot of money to bring in some woman off the streets to put up for sale." She smiles, patting my chest, and not seeming all that sad that Payne is currently cut up into tiny pieces, hanging out in the bar.

"Rig used to take a lot of trips out there back in the day. Payne was a greedy bastard and wanted more money than God. I've heard that the Muerte isn't well-liked around those parts but they have cash flowing in." Lorrie starts to slide her hand down, covering my cock with her palm and frowning when she realizes I'm not hard for her.

Only one woman gets me hard and she's not fucking here. No one can hold a candle to my little bird.

"Thank you for sharing that bit of information. I've always wondered where Payne was disappearing to and where he was getting expensive, pure snow," I say and muse out loud, smacking Lorrie's rubbing palm away and standing suddenly.

She falls to the ground with a pathetic cry and stares up at me with fear as I tower over her frail, weak body.

"I–I can be useful. I'll please you like no other woman has before, you can do whatever you want to my body," she stutters, desperately reaching for my belt buckle as if blowing me will save her life.

"I don't want a willing woman, I'd rather hear her screams as I take her body," I say without emotion, picturing my initials on Tillie's back as I fucked her ass.

I shiver, needing to see her tears and hear her pleas for it all to stop once again. It's been too long and I'm hungry for more of her.

Lorrie's eyes widen as I pull my gun out from the back of my pants and dig the barrel between her eyes. She starts blabbering, promising me she can be all that I want but the thing is... no one can expect little bird.

"Once a whore, always a whore," I say, picturing my birth mother passed out on the threadbare couch as some faceless stranger rammed his cock in her, all for the needle that pierced her skin every night.

My lips twitch at the corners, wanting to smile but I never can. Not unless I force myself to. I pull the trigger and watch as Lorrie's brain matter splatters on the walls in chunks. I take a deep breath, closing my eyes, feeling more alive but not fully. The warm spray of her blood doesn't even cheer up my mood. At least we are finally getting somewhere and we have a destination. Time to make a deal with this Muerte gang with me being the new Prez.

Soon, very fucking soon, she'll be within reach.

CHAPTER 9

Tillie

The front door shutting sounds loud behind me, making my face form a grimace. I'd rather be anywhere else than here but my week is up and I'm back in Franco's house. I already miss sleeping in Dalton's arms and torturing him by sleeping in his T-shirt and nothing else as I snuggle very close to him. He's doing so good even though it's giving him blue balls. I wish I could have stayed at his club, it's so different from the one I grew up in. Don't get me wrong, there are still criminals living under his club roof but everyone treated me with respect. That surprised me. I at least thought I'd be ignored when I started coming out of the bedroom to walk around but the members were actually friendly.

Hell. Even the sweetbutts were nice. Going out of their way, asking if I needed anything. It's such a dramatic change from when I was living with the Demon Jokers, making me stare at everyone like they would have jumped me at any time and forced me to my knees just like old times. It really showed what kind of leader Dalton's dad was and what he will be too. Tomorrow, he's dropping out of school, not that I can blame him. He has too much responsibility at the club and it needs his full focus. I'm going to miss seeing the douchebag at school.

So here the fuck I am. Back and dreading every moment, but I promised myself no more running. I need to plant my feet firmly on the ground and not take shit from anyone. I can let my guard down in the shower when I'm alone, and cry if I want to without anyone seeing. Though I don't think I can go in the kitchen without seeing Dalton bleeding out, Payne with a bullet in his forehead, and Franco taking what was never his.

"Tillie. Please come and join me." Diana's voice comes from the living room and her tone does not sound happy at all.

I wince at her voice and drop my overnight bag by the staircase before heading into the spacious room that speaks of money at first glance. Diana is sitting on the white couch with her back ramrod straight and a whole tea set displayed on the coffee table. She gestures towards the opposite couch without saying anything else. I can't get a read on her emotions, her face is completely blank. My ass hits the cushion and we just stare at each other as she starts making me a cup of tea before passing it over. Drinking in silence is nerve-wracking and I'm beginning to wonder if she poisoned my cup because she's staring so intently at me as I take a drink.

"I don't care what you do in your spare time. You can come and go as you please, spend the money I put in a bank account for you," she says smoothly, setting her teacup down, "spread your legs for whoever you want but you will stay away from my husband, am I clear?"

I nearly choke on the tea, setting the cup down quickly. She got straight to the point, no beating around the bush but I didn't expect anything else.

"Yes," I rasp out, choosing to glance over her shoulder instead of her eyes that show everything she thinks of me.

Trash.

Whore.

Filth.

"Good. Glad we are on the same page. Sugar?" she asks suddenly as she scoops some into her tea and quirks a brow as I shake my head. "I'm happy we could clear the air. I gave birth to you but that doesn't mean I won't kick you to the curb the first chance I get. Franco somewhat thinks of you as a daughter." Her face contorts in disgust before the look quickly vanishes.

I can't blame her for hating me but it still fucking hurts. It seems we are never going to have a mother-daughter relationship. I also highly doubt Franco is looking at me like I'm his daughter. More like an ice cream sundae with a cherry on top. There's something deeply disturbed about him. Every time he glanced at me, it's like he's looking right through me and seeing someone else but that didn't stop his gaze from wandering all over me with longing. I can't help the full body shudder.

"I understand. I won't get in your way. I'm only staying until graduation then I'm leaving." I'm not sure where I'll go, I think college is out of the question for someone like me.

Maybe I'll travel until I'm somewhere with a sense of belonging. That thought sounds lonely though, with no one else around. It wouldn't have bothered me months ago but ever since coming here... I crave to be touched by five possessive guys. Yes. Five. I included Dom. He's a different kind of messed up. I mean... the guy stalked me through the mall but he also seems to take care of those that mean something to him. Because I think I'm beginning to be that something he cares for. Only time will tell.

"I think that's for the best dear. After all, you brought the one person who I've been running from for eighteen years right to my door. I can't imagine who else you're going to have show up out of the blue." She calmly says the words but her fist clenches on her designer dress, a bitter facial expression aimed at me.

I'm beginning to wonder who is worse. Lorrie or Diana. At least Lorrie never pretended to like me. Diana puts on an act in front of others, wishing I never existed. I wonder what awaits Lorrie now that Payne is dead. I hope she gets everything she deserves.

"I'm sorry, I can only imagine how hard it's been for you," I reply back sarcastically but hold back what I really want to say to her. *Fuck you, Diana.* "Payne was never supposed to find me, I don't know how he did so fast." For a split-second, I fear that Cruz is coming for me next but push that thought aside.

He would have shown up when Payne did, right beside him. He doesn't know where I am... I have to believe that. I'd already be chained up somewhere within his grasp if he knew I was here. Sweat gathers at my nape and my hands slightly shake because if Cruz ever finds me... Payne is going to look like a walk in the park compared to that sociopath.

"Payne was always thinking he sat on a pedestal. I should have never answered the door when you showed up. I knew my past would catch up with me eventually," Diana whispers and flicks her hand like she's putting it all behind her.

Just that simple for her.

It hurts. God does it hurt. At least I had Doris as somewhat of a mother figure. She taught me to not cave, to never back down even when men knocked me down, and that men should fall at my feet one day. Use your brain and the body God blessed you with.

Tears gather in the corners of my eyes before I blink them away. I miss Doris. She was always there when I needed someone. She knew I didn't belong at that club. I wonder if she knew who my real father was?

"Who is my father?" I blurt out before I lose my nerves, needing to know and at the same time scared of the answer.

Diana's teacup trembles in her hand moments before she slams it on the coffee table as she glares at me. Her gaze doesn't stay on me long before she looks over my shoulder as if she can't stand to see my face.

"I was young and stupid," she begins, playing with a small mark on the inside of her elbow but quickly pulls her hand away when she notices me watching.

She was hooked on heroin. I would recognize the marks anywhere. I used to serve the needles on trays back at the Demon Jokers' club.

"I grew up in a household that, well, wasn't this." She gestures around, indicating the lavish lifestyle she's made happen for herself. "My parents were drunks and never cared what I did. So, when an older, handsome guy on a motorcycle gave me attention, I took it without looking back. I ran away from home and it was fine at first. I was so naive and foolish. I just wanted to be loved and I thought that Payne was the love of my life." She pauses with a deep breath and looks me deep in my eyes, the color reflecting that of my own.

"You saw his true colors," I state in a low voice. I can only imagine what he did to her to make her so afraid of him, to run away in the middle of the night and never look back.

"That's an understatement. He put on a believable act for a while but eventually, small signs started showing that something wasn't right with him. He wanted me to take drugs, be at his beck and call. He treated me like his prized pet. I learned that it wasn't love but obsession. Everything I wanted went away just like before until the man I had an affair with came into the picture. He showed me such kind-ness. I mean, he was still in a business that had bad people but he had soft spots that drew me in." She clears her throat and reaches for her cup.

I find it hard to breathe. This is it. I'm terrified of what she's going to say. I think deep down I already know who he was but I need to hear the words out loud.

"Who?" I rasp out, my whole body starting to shake.

"My punishment was for loving him and Payne never knew who but I'm guessing he found out the older you got. You look so much like Rig," Diana says so softly as she meets my gaze but her words suddenly sound like I'm under water. The world around me grows dark and I feel alone, as if she's not even in the room sitting across from me.

I distantly hear deep, wheezing gasps, and a sob of a broken heart.

My world tilts as I climb to my feet in a daze, walking past Diana who doesn't say another word. Or maybe she does but I can't hear her over the sobbing. My eyes blur and it hurts to breathe. Stumbling into the kitchen, I keep walking until I find myself in the garage. The sound of sobbing followed me out here, but now it sounds louder, more frantic. It's like I can't escape it. I touch my fingers to my face and they come away wet. Why are my cheeks wet? It takes me a second longer to realize that I'm the one making those awful noises.

Rig.

I grab a fistful of my hair and scream before picking up the nearest object to me. The wrench sails through the air and smashes into an expensive car windshield but I couldn't care less. I want to punch, kick, and break anything in my path. I need an outlet. I need to leave right now before I fall to the garage floor and decide to never get back up. My gaze connects to Logan's crotch rocket in the far corner of the garage. I run past all the ridiculously expensive cars and don't stop until I'm swinging my leg over his bike while backing it out of the garage door. His keys are still inside the engine and

I send a silent prayer that at least I have this moment. I peel so fast out of the driveway that it leaves black marks and smoke billowing out behind me.

With no destination in mind and no helmet, I feel reckless but don't give a shit. The same question keeps going around and around in my head, the answer I've been looking for since I was sixteen.

Why?

Why did Rig leave?

Why did he leave me behind?

I take a corner too sharp and my knee skims against the asphalt hard enough to tear my jeans but I quickly straighten out and concentrate on the road once more. Or at least as best as I can under the circumstances. Did Rig not want me? Did he know I was his daughter? He had to. Never once did I feel like I wasn't loved in his presence. He took care of me until one day he didn't.

Where is he?

Is he still even alive?

Oh God. Payne knew. He knew about Rig.

My breath stalls and it hurts so bad, like I'll never be able to draw in another proper breath without it being painful. Driving dangerously isn't helping, I need a different outlet where I can get lost. It feels like I've been driving aimlessly for hours, I don't even know what part of town I'm in. By the looks of things, it's not the best area with buildings looking like they're falling apart and I'm pretty sure I just passed a hooker on the corner street. I see a bright pink neon sign ahead and speed up without a second thought until I'm pulling into the parking lot. It's a shitty parking lot with potholes and a building that has no windows, only a solid, black door.

It doesn't matter that it's the afternoon. Strip clubs will always have people coming and going at all hours of the day.

The heavy door slams shut behind me, and it takes my eyes a second to adjust to the low lights and strobe lights flashing around the stage, making it easy to see the few men crowded around the platform. The smell of cheap alcohol, sweet perfume, and sex fills the air. A sad, familiar presence of the atmosphere makes my shoulders inch down a notch from their present tightness. It's really fucking pathetic that of all places, I feel more comfortable here because I'm used to this. Greed, lust, and more greed. It brings back the memories of the first time I stepped foot in the strip club the Demon Jokers owned.

"Tillie. Look at me child." Doris pulled my attention away from the woman sitting on a man's lap, grinding on him as he played with her breasts.

I looked at Doris with wide eyes, feeling sweat coat the back of my neck. I felt sick. The basement stayed in the darkest part of my mind but any little thing could trigger my panic attacks. It's been only a few months and yet it feels like it just happened yesterday. I kept my head down, stayed quiet, and did as I was told. It was the only thing that was helping me to survive and Doris being here for me. Payne saw me as weak and he left me alone for the most part, he didn't think I was worth his time. He told everyone to leave me alone as long as I learned my place.

Apparently, he felt like dancing for strange men would keep me in place. He's right. I'll do anything at this point so I won't have a repeat of being brutally... raped.

That word. Rape. That one word is hard to even think about. I fucking hate it.

It's vile. A disease eating away at me. It's just another word but to some, like me, it brings back every bad thing that was done to me.

"You can do this. Remember what I said. Those wings that are broken and hurting right now, it won't always be that way. We have to start on the ground but we can make it to the top if we

never give up. I'm going to show you how. Men can easily be controlled, it starts with that dick between their legs." Doris nodded towards the black, glittery stage as a woman danced topless around a pole.

Men leaned forward in their seats, eyes never straying from her as she swirled slowly around the pole in almost a seductive way. They never noticed the one waitress going from table to table collecting drinks and her hand as she stole money from their pockets as she rubbed up against them.

I saw it all. My breath held for her because I thought she would get caught but not once did the men notice. All their attention was centered solely on the platform and the way the stripper's body moved to the beat of the music.

I turned to Doris and gulped loudly, straightening my spine. I wanted that kind of power over men with a burning desire so hot it felt like my insides were on fire. I needed to be that woman who showed no fear. Who could wield control with her body. It's all I had felt. I had to try.

"Show me."

I remember the words leaving my mouth and the fond, yet proud smile Doris gave me. I didn't know it at the time but she was right. She was teaching me that broken pieces can be put back together and come back stronger than ever.

"I'm not serving you alcohol. You shouldn't be here and don't even try to tell me you're twenty-one. I've been in this business a long time. Get outta here." The raspy, chain-smoker voice startles me and has me swirling around to see an older lady behind the bar wiping down glasses.

"If I wanted a drink, I could have gone to the liquor store up the street. A flash of boobs in this part of town will get you just about anything, even under the drinking age," I reply back with a shrug and lean against the bar as I stare her in the eyes, willing my startled heart to calm down.

"Forget it. I'm not hiring. I don't need the cops at my place again." She raises a brow, looking me up and down.

"I'm eighteen and I'm not looking for a job. I just want to dance for a little while. I'll let you keep all the money I make too. The cops won't be a problem, trust me." I can't stop myself from rolling my eyes at the thought of the cops showing up here.

What are they going to do? I'm eighteen and I'm deep in Franco's clutches just as they are. I hold back a shiver and wait for her to give me an answer as she finishes stacking drinking glasses behind the bar. She swings her towel over her shoulder and leans her elbows on the smooth, wood surface of the bar.

"Hundred percent of your profits and any tips. No sex in my club, got it? I recognize that look you have on your face right now, seen it plenty of times in my dancers eyes. Sometimes the thing we hate the most is all we know and a way to block out everything else. Get up there next song and leave when I say your time is up." She nods and dismisses me without another word.

I don't stick around for her to change her mind or for the next set for one of the girls to start before I can get up there. I head to the back of the dressing room, passing naked strippers as I stride towards a set of lockers and act like I belong here. Hell. I do belong in this strip club. It really is all I know. I chuck the motorcycle keys and my shoes in the locker, not even hesitating to unzip my pants. I'm not one for being shy about my body and don't care who is staring at me. I ignore my phone going off like crazy and shut the locker without answering. I know it's one of the guys and I'm not telling them where I'm at. Once I'm down to just my underwear, I yank my hair out of its ponytail and shake it out. Clad in only a red, lacy thong and matching bra that Dom bought me, I walk out of the room until I'm standing behind a black curtain.

The mutter of the men out there is low and the music loud, a seductive song to dance to beats through the strip club. A topless girl passes me and winks as she strides off stage while counting a handful of bills. The music changes to Rihanna's *Pour it up* and that tells me it's my cue.

Standing on my toes, I part the curtain and walk slowly to the beat with a sway in my hips towards the pole while running my hands through my hair and down the curves of my body. Before I make it to the pole, I quickly drop to my knees and spin with my hands grazing the floor behind me. The position leaves my back arched, head tilted back as I lean farther back and I bounce my body up and down on the back of my heels while keeping my knees spread wide. I shake my hair out so it's a wild mess of locks before dragging a finger down the center of my chest and end up moving my whole body forward to the stage floor. My chest presses into the floor as I slide slightly forward until my ass is sticking in the air. I slowly move my legs apart and end up in the splits. I can feel eyes on me and shouts from the center floor but I don't look. I keep my eyes on the lights until it's blinding and creates black dots to dance in my vision. I'm here to dance and forget, not to see greed in the eyes of men. Ignoring everything, I get to my hands and knees and crawl towards the pole with a few hair flips while my back is arched. Grabbing the cold metal, I grip it with both hands and slowly rise to my feet while leaning back and dropping halfway down before sliding back up with my whole body plastered to the pole. Doing a small spin around the pole with one leg wrapped around it, my muscles hold me up as I free my hands to lean all the way back until my hair is grazing the stage. Straightening up once more, I grip tight with both hands and jump while I flip upside down on the pole. My legs slowly spread until I'm doing a Jade, the splits in the air as I gaze down at the floor. All the blood rushes to my head and I stay like that for a few seconds before bending forward to wrap my right thigh around the pole. My other leg straightens in the air, skimming the pole and I twirl around the slippery metal with my hands free, sliding down inch by inch. I flip at the last second until my feet are touching the ground again. Taking a deep breath, I circle the pole while dancing to the beat of the new song playing

Thoughts of Rig fly through my mind as my body keeps moving on autopilot. For years, I thought Rig up and left me behind to get out of the club but I think I've been wrong this whole time. Once you're in, that's it. You die on your bike servicing the club or you get taken out. I think in the pit of my gut I know deep down that he's not alive. I think I've known since he first disappeared. He was the only one who ever treated me like I was a somebody. He taught me everything I needed to know, tuning up a car, helping with my homework, and offering advice when I needed it the most. He was always protecting me from the harshness of the club life. That whole time... he was treating me like his daughter. I just never knew that he was my father.

Why did he never tell me?!

My father.

I'm not sure how long I've been dancing up here or when I'm going to be kicked out. It leaves my muscles tight with the way I have to have a strong grip on the pole but it's relaxing at the same time. Something I'm used to doing without a second thought, an easy escape.

At one point, I decide to leave the pole and move towards the front of the stage to collect more money for the owner who I'm pretty sure is the bartender. Most people might have just kicked me to the curb but she knew I needed this. It's the least I can do for her. I haven't looked out at the small crowd the whole entire time I was up here but I think making some eye contact might help bring more dollars to the stage. The Weeknd starts playing and I find it's easy to dance to his songs, they always feel seductive and exactly like sex.

Hot and sweaty. Rhythmic.

I don't know why but men love it when you crawl to them. It always brought more money to the stage. It could be the submissive position or being on my knees but it works for me each and every time. At the edge of the stage, on my hands and knees, I lean back again and don't stop until my back is sliding against the stage. Bringing my legs towards and spreading them wide open until they make the perfect V, I lean up on my elbows while looking forward.

I freeze at the sight before me, my breath stalling in my chest. I should have realized how quiet it's been for a while. No more catcalls, hollers, just the music.

Fuck.

"Don't stop on my account. Keep dancing," Nicky says, leaning back in his seat and skimming his index finger back and forth over his lips as his emerald green eyes trail over my position.

When there is one, the others are never far behind.

Double fuck.

CHAPTER 10

Nicky

Tillie is fucking lucky that I'm a man who can control his anger and has the patience of a saint.

"Are you listening to me, son? As my heir, I expect better from you." Jin guzzles his bottle of water and hands it off to one of his minions while tightening his Do-Ji uniform before standing in the middle of the mat.

I grind my teeth, breathing hard as I receive a text from Logan that Tillie is not at the house. I'll deal with it in a second. I throw my phone to the corner of the mat without a second look and approach my father in the middle of the black mat with the dragon symbol of the triad. I stand perfectly straight, waiting for him to begin and try to not worry about Tillie pulling a disappearing act.

I can't show emotions in front of my father. He likes to destroy anything that holds my interest. I learned at a young age to never show what I'm thinking. Keeping a neutral facial expression hides all my secrets.

The faster I can kick his ass, the faster I can get out of here to go give Tillie a spanking. She's just begging for it.

God. She really does test my patience but holding back makes it all worth it in the end. Gratification is key.

"I hear you, Sir." I bow in respect as he does the same back but respect is the last thing I have for this monster.

One of his minions standing off the mat yells out fight in Japanese and I form my body into a relaxed state while making sure my muscles are ready to move. The fight stance requires my feet spread with one foot forward and my elbows bent while my fingers are perfectly straight. Jin yells, striking out fast with his left foot. His hit almost connects with my temple but I duck fast enough that he misses. Swinging my right hand out, the side of my palm connects with the side of his body, right against his ribs.

Jin lets out a whoosh of breath and bounces back on his feet, his eyes narrowed on me with concentration as we circle each other. We go back and forth, moving forward as we try to take down one another. Jabs and kicks continue until sweat is coating my chest but I can't show that I'm getting tired. I sweep my foot out, bending down low, and aim to hook it around his ankle to bring him down. Jin's body hits the mat with a thud before he moves quickly out of the way as I try to slam the side of my foot across his neck. He rolls across the mat and ends in a crouch with a smile.

"What have I taught you, Nicholas?" Jin taunts and charges at me, faking a left, high kick but he swings his fist at the same time to connect with my stomach.

A breath leaves my chest with a grunt and I don't have time to duck out of the way as his other fist connects with my cheek, grazing on the corner of my lips. Down on my knees, Jin stands over me as I pant and stare at his feet without looking up at him.

He grabs my hair, forcing me to glance up, and starts laughing with a shake of his head.

"No mercy, son. There is honor in our culture. We fight karate with respect but you need to learn to play dirty." Jin makes a tsking noise in the back of his throat and shoves me in disgust as he strides off the mat.

I spit out blood, wiping my arm across my mouth and watching it come away red as it leaves a smear on the white, Do-Ji uniform. I've been fighting with Jin since I was a kid right on these mats. He's been training me but he never wants me to beat him. That would make him look weak and he can't lead the triad in my peoples' eyes if his son can beat him. It means I'm stronger. When that day comes, he won't stare at me like I'm a disgrace. He'll look at me with fear when I end his life and take over the triad. I can't wait for that day to come. Soon.

"We have precious cargo coming in two nights and an auction the following weekend. I expect you there and your little pet. She can keep my clients happy before bidding starts." Jin turns his head to me and I smooth my face into a calm mask before he can see the rage all over my face.

"Of course, Father." I bow to him and wait until he grunts and leaves the room.

I gnash my teeth together. He can see through my disguise, I can feel it. He knows that I have feelings for my toy. I jog over to my phone with a grimace, moving my jaw back and forth as it starts to swell.

I feel like I'm going to explode, all this pent-up energy just waiting to explode. I always have to hide my true feelings behind a blank expression. Always hiding. Keeping everything deep down inside. My app finally opens to Tillie's location and I feel my eyes widen at the place she's at.

My palm is twitching already and I can picture her ass jiggling from each smack of my hand.

Why the hell is she at a strip club in the seediest part of town?!

I barely remember changing or hopping in my car as I raced towards the highway strip and pulled into the parking lot of *Girls, Girls, and Girls* strip club. I texted the group chat and knew the guys wouldn't be too far behind me. The moment I stride through the door, my gaze goes right to the stage. The very second I laid eyes on her, I know every fucker in here is going to die for staring at what's ours.

Is it possible to be furious and enchanted at the same time? Like I want to shout, maybe lock her in a room, but at the same time I want to fuck her into the mattress. She has us all wrapped around her finger and doesn't even know it. I'm not a good man, never will be. I've done shit that can't be undone and I have no regrets about what I've had to do in life to survive the abuse of Jin.

All I want to do when she opens that sassy mouth is shove my cock down her throat again until she shuts up. I love the fire that burns in her eyes and the dark thoughts that flash across her face. The way she glares but clenches her thighs at the same time. I'm very observant and love to watch her emotions flicker from hate to need in a split-second. She's just as messed up as we are and I like that. I want that. I want *her*. A woman who can hold her own and give as much as we throw at her. We don't need a Paris who laps up attention like a fucking poodle. I want a fucking pit bull woman with a bite.

Tillie would tear me into pieces with her teeth if she really wanted to but she doesn't. When something has been programmed into your life for so long, it's all you know. You live and breathe it. For us, that's pleasure and pain. It all goes hand in hand.

"Hey! I'm calling the cops!" a woman behind the bar threatens with a shotgun when she sees me taking off my jacket to throw on the bar top and notices the guns tucked into the front of my pants.

I reach over quickly and snatch it out of her hands while

unloading the shot slugs with a flick of my wrist. She's about to open her mouth until she sees the greens flipping through my hands. I shut her up by throwing a couple G's on the bar.

"No, you're not. Give us an hour. That girl is ours." I nod my head towards the stage and the woman glances around with a gulp and nods her head while collecting the money. She takes one last look at Tillie before she runs towards the back room.

I roam my gaze around the club after she disappears, counting five men that I have to kill tonight but what has me raising a brow in surprise is when my eyes clash with Dom across the strip club.

He's coming through the back exit with a damn Mk-16 rifle casually hanging from his hand as he surveys the room. His eyes meet mine at the same time and he smirks while gesturing towards the five men crowded around the stage as Tillie twirls around the pole with her eyes closed.

I tilt my head, wondering what his game is but decide it doesn't hurt to have someone who can help get rid of bodies at the moment. I'll repeatedly stab him in the gut if he tries anything that would cause harm to Tillie. I give a single nod to him and walk with my hands in my pants pocket as I go to stand behind a fucker looking at our girl.

Yeah. I said it. *Our* girl. I'm not an idiot. I see the way Dom is watching her. Clear as day, I can tell he wants her as he looks her up and down with dark eyes that burn with desire and possessiveness. Tillie didn't seem the least bit concerned that he's been stalking her. I know about that too because I hacked into his phone. It's almost laughable how easy you can hack into anyone's phone. Picture after picture of her fills his photo gallery every single day. I'm going to have to talk to Dalton about his security issue. The fuck face even has a picture of her sleeping at the club in Dalton's bed... with him cuddled right up to her in his sleep. Not sure how he got by everyone that patrols the compound. Gotta admit, even I'm impressed. I should be pissed about this situation but for the life of me, I can't find it in me to be. Danger seems to follow Tillie wherever she goes, so having another pair of eyes on her won't hurt. Currently, Dom looks like he's going to open fire round after round at the salivating men staring at all the skin she's showing.

I get it, I really do, but her body isn't for anyone else. Hell, I get mad when another guy breathes in the same room as her. It's such a strange feeling she causes within me. It's either strangle her for disobeying me or fuck her stupid until she only screams *yes*. Since I kind of like having her around, I'll go with option two.

"Get out." I keep my voice low, keeping my eyes on the stage so I don't miss anything Tillie is doing, and pick the guy out of his seat by the collar of his shirt without glancing at him.

"Hey! Who the hell do you thin–" he stutters but shuts up when I look him in the eye and don't say anything. "Yeah, you got it, man." He must see the murder in my eyes for looking at what is mine and it fucking pisses me off that I even had to take my eyes off her to tell this fuckwad to get out.

I toss him aside and take his seat, kicking my feet up on the table. It gives me a view right in the center of the stage. Another man stares at me, frozen with a glass halfway to his mouth and I only have to raise a brow before he's scattering to the exit. Dom cleared out the other section and comes to sit next to me, placing his rifle on the table while getting relaxed. Tillie hasn't noticed the empty strip club, she seems to be in her own little world. That's okay. I could watch her dance forever.

"Beautiful," Dom's voice comes out a low whisper of awe and completely ruptured, staring at Tillie as she runs her hands down the curve of her breasts to her sexy hips.

I'm not sure if he's talking to me or himself. I can't help but agree though.

"That rose has thorns," I tell him without looking away as Tillie grips the pole and slowly twirls around it.

That color of red on her is alluring and incredibly sexy.

"Are you trying to warn me? I don't see how that's a bad thing. I don't mind bleeding to have something so beautiful and delicate in my hands." Dom hums in appreciation as she gets to her knees and starts crawling towards the front of the stage.

I feel my pants getting tighter, my cock straining against my zipper, and I know Tey is going to lose his mind when he gets here. I'm going to have to zip tie him up, he'll take one look at Tillie and want to impregnate her right here and now. He won't care that he's pumping her full of his little swimmers in a seedy strip club. Tey... he would be content with knowing little Teys would be planting roots and Tillie would be stuck with him.

"Fuck, man. I can't take this kind of torture," Dalton mutters behind me with a groan and sits his ass next to me, cursing as he watches Tillie dance exotically.

I don't bother responding. I know Logan and Tey arrive at the same time when the barely there sound of the door slamming shut is heard over the music but you can't hear their approach. You get used to stealing, breaking and entering, killing people... you get real good at being fucking quiet when you want to be.

"Logan, please. I'm begging you," Tey practically whimpers as Tillie crawls closer to the edge and leans back with her legs spread wide.

Her skin is smooth as caramel but riddled with scars and tattoos that I'd like to nibble on while she's tied up to my bed and at my mercy. I can understand the desperation Tey is feeling right now. It's like a forbidden fruit dangling in front of your face, but then again I've always taken what I wanted. I would spend hours between her juicy thighs, enjoying the sweet torture of wringing out orgasm after orgasm out of her. Watching her squirt all over, soaking my face until I'm drowning in her. My fingers twitch across my bottom lip, resisting the urge to bring her off the stage and dragging her across my lap until her ass is red and blistering. She happens to look up as dark, delicious thoughts cross my mind and I enjoy the way her eyes widen as she draws in a sharp breath.

It's like I'm taking away all her oxygen and only releasing her when it suits me. I want to give her life and be able to take it away when I want to.

"Don't stop on my account. Keep dancing." I stare into her dark eyes that spark with pain and anger all at once.

Her emotions always cross her face like a rolling film, flicker after flicker of what she's feeling. Easy to read and making it hard to hide secrets from me. I like uncovering secrets, ones that can hurt a person, and tie them to me until I let them free. I don't even have to try with her, she's an open book.

She looks hesitant, refusing to look away from me but comes to a decision when she just aims a glare at me.

"Ah. There's that spark. Dance for us, mama," Dom orders from across the table, leaning back with a grin as Tillie whips her gaze over to him with disbelief crossing her face.

"What the fuck?" Logan growls somewhere off to my left, probably just now noticing Dom.

I look at Logan over my shoulder with a small head shake, seeing his lips curled in a snarl like he wants to take a chunk out of Dom with his bare teeth. Can't say I blame him. It would solve the problem of him trying to take Tillie away from us, but Dom knows things that are coming to light. The hard drive Logan gave me from Franco's computer was disturbing to say the least and it's getting harder and harder to decide who to trust.

"Lo, not here." It's the only thing I say in a hard voice.

He narrows his eyes at me before glancing up at the ceiling with a muttered curse and shakes off Tey who was holding him back from attacking Dom like a wild animal. Logan turns his gaze to Tillie as she crouches on the stage, looking between all of us warily.

"Finish the song, baby girl. Afterwards, we need to have that talk, okay?" Logan says stiffly, grabbing her chin so she looks at him.

She closes her eyes as if in pain and nods her head before pulling away. I hate that look on her face. It makes my body tighten, having the urge to go find whoever hurt her and kill them. We are the only ones allowed to cause her suffering so at the end of the day, we can change that expression to one of pleasure.

I let out a grunt as Tey sits his tight, muscular ass on my thigh, distracting me, and places his unicorn on the table facing the stage. The sight causes me to smile until I quickly wipe it off my face when I notice Dom glancing at us with his head tilted.

"What the fuck are you looking at?" I say harshly, reaching slowly into my back pocket for my throwing stars.

I'll end him for fucking judging us. Anything or anyone that wants to hurt Tey, I'll make them stop breathing. It's that simple

"You do you, man. Love is love." Dom salutes me with his fingers and puts his digits in his mouth, whistling loudly in a catcall when Tillie starts flipping her hair while bouncing on the back of her heels.

The position causes Tey to moan and bite his fist before he looks back at me with a heated gaze. I take my hand away from my back pocket and decided to let Dom go from that very close call to death. The stories of his father and him... I think he was right at the rave. Maybe not all is as it seems. There's more Dom knows but he's holding his cards close. I can respect that but time is ticking because Tillie already got hurt in our care by Payne and I need to know who else might come for her so I can protect what's mine. I'll find the answers eventually with or without his support. It really is all Logan's call but if he can protect those he cares about, he'll do it. Case in point when Tillie was staying with Dalton for the week. I may not approve of his actions but I know why he did it. It's going to backfire for him, maybe all of us when Tillie finds out about Paris.

"Nicholas, can you picture it? I've been wanting to paint her in blood, seeing all that skin soaking wet in red. I wonder how she's going to feel when we take her together. It's going to be a fucking tight fit having two cocks sliding in that pussy at the same time, but she can take it. I might need to record it, something to jerk off later to on lonely nights." Tey talks really fast, his gaze not once moving from the stage until he hears me choking on absolutely nothing.

"Jesus, Tey. Not here... but tell me later in the car." I keep my voice low, not looking at him but I want every filthy whispered word coming out of his mouth until my zipper bursts open from my hard as steel cock.

I could whip it out right now and use it as a weapon if need be. I'm so painfully hard that I can feel the vein pulsing with my heartbeat and the tip of my cock leaking with pre cum.

Tey chuckles darkly and stands up to disappear around the stage somewhere. To do what? I have no clue. You just never know with him.

"It's about time, Nicky. Stop holding back, brother. It's going to eat away at you and eventually you'll have regrets. Screw everyone else. Jin can talk business but he can't control who you love. If he interferes, we'll take care of it," Dalton says in a gravelly voice next to me and pats my shoulder before swearing under his breath and getting out of his seat.

I clear my throat, gripping the wood chair armrests, and try to control my breathing. Fuck. I love them like family, more than blood. He's right, but being Jin's son puts everyone close to me in danger. That's the only reason I agreed with Logan about the Paris situation. It got both our fathers off our backs. The whole thing was done behind Tey and Dalton's back. I can see this not ending up good for any of us but I still wouldn't change anything.

"Tey! Get your ass off the stage! Put your goddamn shirt back on," Dalton shouts from the side of the stage, laughing his ass off as Tey struts down the stage like a runway model without his shirt towards a giggling Tillie.

"Hey, muffin. You look so sexy. I know I promised to fuck you when you're bleeding but I'm having a hard time not whipping out my cock and giving you all my cum right now. Do you think it will be a boy or girl?!" Tey asks excitedly just as the music ends, making his announcement really loud as the soundtrack dies off.

"Tey!" Tillie places her hands on her thick thighs, her shoulders shaking with her head bowed.

The laughter that comes out of her mouth sounds off, too loud until we all notice at the same time the tears silently tracking down her cheeks when she glances up under the purple lights.

"Who the fuck hurt you? I'll cut off their hand and make them fuck their cock with the severed limb," Tey says seriously, his body partially vibrating as he helps her off the floor and envelopes her in his arms.

"I need a drink. I–I can't do this sober. It's been a horrible day, more so than usual." Tillie wipes at her tears, giving Tey a watery smile as she leans up to place a small kiss on his cheek then walks away behind the stage to put her clothes back on.

"What was that about?" Logan demands, his fists clenched and his gaze swinging towards me with a worried expression.

I shake my head. She doesn't know about Paris. I think we'd see a lot more rage from her if that was the case. Something else, other than us, hurt her today.

"She was fine when I dropped her off at your house. You should know since you were there." Dalton glares at Logan, folding his big arms over his chest.

"I was until Franco needed me at the station. I had to switch out more drugs. This is getting ridiculous. I was on my way back when you texted that she was at my house, I knew Franco wasn't there. Diana was home but retired to her room, something about needing to rest." Logan's brows are furrowed, his voice angry and just as confused as the rest of us.

"Obviously, something did happen. She usually shrugs things off her shoulders, even after everything we've thrown at her. Instead, she comes to this trashy strip club to dance like she needed an escape. She's crying, for fuck's sake," I interrupt them, pondering what could have happened to get her this upset.

"She wants a drink and I'm guessing she doesn't want to go back to your place, Russo." Dom gets to his feet, slinging his rifle strap so it rests against his back before turning to Dalton. "And I'm not letting her back in that club of yours until you up your security. Get some fucking cameras. I've watched you snuggle her in bed for days and you didn't even know I was there," Dom finishes with a disgusted shake of his head before glaring at all of us.

"What?!" Dalton yells in a booming voice, advancing

towards Dom with a pissed off expression like he's going to beat the shit out of him.

Two shows in one night. How did I get so lucky?

"Stop it!" Tillie screams loudly behind us, making us all turn towards her as she stands by the exit with her fists on her hips and, unfortunately, fully dressed.

That glare on her face makes me want to smack her ass all the more. As if he can read my thoughts, Tey glances at me with a wicked smirk. He knows my need for control and I would like nothing better than to have Tillie under my control until she's begging for me to fuck her sweet pussy.

I love a good beggar. Kneeling with hopeful eyes staring up at me like I'm her God she's praying to. I'll answer all her prayers with the tip of my tongue on her skin and my cock buried deep inside of her.

"What the fuck do you suggest, Dom?" Logan sneers, walking towards Tillie and placing his body in front of her until she pushes him from behind and kicks the back of his knee.

Logan's eyes widen as he stumbles slightly and he glances at Tillie as she walks around him to stand beside him instead of behind him. My lips twitch and her gaze flashes towards mine for a hot second with a smirk before it's wiped from her face again.

"Can we please stop acting like children and just get along for at least a little while?" Tillie stares at all of us, meeting each of our gazes until she receives a small nod that we agree to behave.

"Baby girl..." Logan tries a different angle with her and I wish him Godspeed.

Never stand in the way of a woman when she sasses you like you're beneath her. If she walks on water, you get the fuck out of her way before she decides to drown you and walks over your corpse.

"Don't you baby girl me, Lo. Enough is enough. I'm done with all this bullshit. Either stand beside me or let me walk away. I've just had... I'm so tired. It never stops." She looks away, blinking her eyes rapidly, and takes a deep breath.

"You're not going anywhere. Don't you know by now that we will follow you and set the world on fire until you're back in our grasp? But if you want to leave, then I dare you to try," Logan challenges with narrowed eyes and steps closer towards her, about to grab her until Dom clears his throat.

"My club is empty until tonight since it's still early. You can get your drink there, mama. No one is going to rush you," Dom declares, making it a threat as he swings his rifle around and unclips the safety while staring us all down, daring anyone to argue with him.

I think he would kill us all and take Tillie for himself but if he's been stalking her then he knows that she may somewhat care for us. She may not trust us completely but there's something there. If she didn't want us in some manner, then she wouldn't have cared that Dalton got stabbed or that Tey's stuffed animal got decapitated. All of this is new for each of us and we are just kind of winging it as we go. She won't ever be alone again, I'm here for the long wild ride that is Tillie. We've shown her that we aren't good men, never will be, and have never promised to be... I think she accepts that because she hasn't gone running for the hills.

"Ok–okay. Tha–that sounds nice," she stutters at Dom, obviously scared to clear the air between us all. That's fine because there will be no more secrets. It's time she let us in to help her. She turns to Logan and grips his jacket sleeve, staring up at him with pleading eyes. "Please? For me? You at least can play nice. It's time, Lo."

Logan gazes down at her, his expression twisting in anger until it clears as he runs a hand through his hair.

"Fine. But she rides with me. We'll follow you," Logan

announces and grabs Tillie's wrist, heading outside before anyone can argue with him.

I don't think anyone will. He's acting like a territorial caveman right now, has been since Franco had his tongue shoved up in Tillie's cunt. If Logan wasn't like a brother, I would have already killed his father without blinking but timing is everything. Jin's days are numbered too. Only a matter of time until I take over the triad and make some changes.

"I'll ride with you." Tey's voice goes deeper, low with seduction and he has a crazed smile stretching across his plump lips as he grabs his unicorn.

I shake my head and follow after him, tapping Dalton's knuckles before he walks over to his motorcycle. I never know what Tey is going to throw at me. Everything is still new to me, about coming out of this shell I've been hiding in the whole time we've been friends. I know it's the same for Tey even though he's more out there than me. He's never afraid of anything. It just scares me that one day it's all going to blow up in my face for loving him and he'll get hurt. My mood darkens as I start the car and follow out behind Dalton.

"About what I said earlier. Can you picture it, Nicky, or am I the only one feeling something that really isn't there?" Tey leans his seat back farther and turns his head towards me.

"It's not that. I feel it all. You. Tillie. I'm just having a hard time. I can't let anything hurt you guys," I confess quietly in the silence of the car.

I'm supposed to be the quiet one of our group, lock everything up inside until I'm choking on it, and do anything to keep my family safe.

Tey doesn't say anything but I can feel his gaze on me as I stare straight ahead while driving. The leather seats creak as he shifts in his seat and his strong grip on my thigh makes me jump a little.

"You trust me?" he asks, his eerie, light blue eyes staring hard into mine when I take a second to glance over at him.

"With my life," I reply back easily before looking back out the window.

"Good. Don't take your eyes off the road and just feel okay?" Tey leans over the console and skims his nose along my neck with a deep inhale.

I swallow thickly and give him a small nod as my head leans over to give him more space. My eyes are on the road but it's almost like I don't even see it. All my focus is on Tey.

The cold brush of his lip ring glides partially over my collarbone as he sucks softly at my neck before biting down hard enough to bruise my pounding pulse. His fingers squeeze my thigh before letting go and gliding towards the button and zipper of my slacks. My breath quickens and my eyes glance down for a second before he bites my neck harder. My gaze snaps back to the road with a curse, my chest expanding on a deep inhale as I try to relax.

"Enjoy this, Nicholas. This is always for you and only you. I don't have a need to touch another man. It's always just going to be the three of us," he whispers along my neck, his pierced tongue sliding up to my earlobe with a long lick that makes me shudder.

The sound of my zipper lowering is loud to my own ear, and my stomach clenches as his fingertips graze my abs and he unsnaps my pants button. The car jerks before I'm able to straighten the wheel as his long fingers wrap around my hard length, pulling me out. His dark chuckle makes me groan, vibrating on my skin and making me feel hot as he moves his hand slowly up and down my cock. I quickly look over at him when he moves away from my neck and his heated gaze doesn't waver from mine as he leans his head back on the headrest with a lazy smile.

"You like that?" he asks and I can only nod as I try not to

crash the car. "Then you're going to love this." He gives that small warning before his hand disappears and is back before I can ask him what he means.

I grunt deeply in my throat and grip the steering wheel even tighter until my knuckles are white. The feeling of his wet hand as he jerks his fist up and down has me peeking down to see his bright red blood smearing down the whole length of my cock. He grins devilishly as I glance up quickly to look at him, seeing him putting his knife away after cutting his palm. The feel of his fingers gripping me tightly, moving faster and faster up and down has me close to the edge in a matter of seconds. My gaze flicks back to the road, trying not to crash as he gives me a hand job.

"I can't wait to feel my cock sliding through Tillie's juicy cunt right alongside yours. It's going to be so tight and wet, she's going to be screaming our names out in a prayer for more." Tey moans deeply in his throat with approval as my cock pulses, imagining exactly that.

The feeling of her walls squeezing us at the same time will be pure heaven with Tey's thick cock sliding smoothly and soaking wet against mine.

"Fuck. Fuck, Tey. Do that again. Squeeze me harder," I grind out through my teeth with a hiss of intense pleasure as he twists his wrist and squeezes around the tip of my cock.

"Look at that." Tey's breathing comes out hard the faster he jerks me off. "My blood, your big cock weeping... you're close to coming, aren't you?" He chuckles when I moan in fucking need after taking my eyes off the road to glance back down at my lap.

He's right. The sight of his blood smeared down my length, covering half of my tattoo, of the dragon's tail, has the tip of my cock leaking pre cum in white drips that slide down to mix with his blood. My thigh muscles tense and my hips come off the seat as I hiss between my teeth. Ribbons of cum shoot up from my pulsing cock, covering Tey's hand and my stomach until I'm completely drained. I lean my head back on the headrest, breathing heavily as I try to focus on the road and not kill us.

"You made this mess, now lick it clean." I gesture towards my lap.

It will be worth the torture when I'm fucking him and Tillie into the mattress.

I don't look but I hear the sound of the leather seat crinkling as he leans over my lap and I feel his hot breath on my abs before the first sweep of his tongue. He licks me slowly with a pleased hum, teasing me as my stomach clenches each time I feel his tongue piercing. I just came but I'm still so fucking hard. My whole body seizes up, my foot slipping on the gas pedal as he suddenly takes my cock between his plump lips and moves all the way down to the base of my dick. He hums around my cock, his nose skimming along my pelvic bone and making goosebumps spread over my whole body. I grunt as he slides his mouth back up my length at a leisurely pace that almost has me driving us off the road until I straighten the wheel. He cleans the last of my cum off the tip of my cock with one swipe of his tongue before sitting back in his seat with a dark chuckle as I glance down angrily at my hard cock wrapped in his fist once more. I could probably punch through a wall alone with just my dick, that's how hard it is. It's red, almost angry looking, and bouncing on my stomach with a slap as he lets go of me.

"Fuck me. That was hot, Nicholas. I'm wondering if I should save all of your cum to shove up our girl's sweet cunt? Maybe we'll have little Nicky's swimmers doing its job and I'll have her barefoot in the kitchen, or torture room, and pregnant in no time." My lips twitch with a barely there smile as I catch my breath with a deep inhale. When I stop at a red light, I glance over at him and see him licking the palm of his hand until only two fingers remain coated with my cum and his blood.

He really is twisted inside his head but I wouldn't have him any other way.

"I'm pretty sure she would kill you if you put a child in her. Now, put my cock away, and don't think I won't forget this. If anyone's in charge here, Tey, it's me. You'll have your punishment when you least expect it," I warn him, already thinking about tying him to the bed with Japanese bondage ropes but shake my head to clear the image away as we pull into a parking lot behind the rest of the guys.

"I'll hold you to that. I didn't know Dom owned this club. Lo and I were here about two months ago before we got rid of that evidence at the precinct." Tey gestures towards the building in front of us and gets out of the car with a smirk as he glances around for Tillie.

You wouldn't think Diablo was a nightclub during the day with its simple, black brick building and empty parking lot right downtown.

"Peaches. Come here for a second." Tey crooks his two fingers covered in my cum and we watch Tillie sway her sassy ass towards us.

CHAPTER 11

Tillie

My hands ache. They feel stiff and tight in spots from wringing them in my lap on the ride over. Logan let me have my peace and his comfortable silence helped knowing that he was right next to me. I'm about to open the flood gates and there's no going back from that. I don't even know if I'm ready but no more.

No more secrets. No more lies. No more running.

It's time to clear everything off my chest and tell my story. Hopefully they won't look at me differently or tell me to pack my bags once they know everything about me.

I'm damaged goods, I'll always have a piece of something missing inside me from all the shit life has taken from me. You can't replace what was taken from me, no matter how much you wish you could.

Logan cuts the engine as we pull into a paved parking lot and breaks the silence when neither of us says anything. "Whatever happens, just know that you're one of us now. We all have to prove ourselves in blood and I think you've done enough of that. You won't bleed anymore, baby girl. I'll kill anyone who tries, except Tey."

"I've been bleeding for a long time, Lo. That's sweet of you but I can handle myself. Let's just see how you feel after I tell you everything." My voice is low and raspy, my throat already closing tight.

I quickly climb out of the car, taking a deep breath while turning my face up to the sun. Why is it only when I'm outside, feeling my skin heat and a light breeze caressing my face, that I feel somewhat free?

"Peaches. Come here for a second." Tey's throaty voice practically purrs, a dark seduction I'm not immune to.

I glance around and find him a few cars behind, climbing out of Nicky's car with a satisfied smirk. That smirk of his is dangerous. You can't tell if he plans on killing you, cutting up your body into little pieces, and tossing them into the ocean to feed the fishes. Or... if he plans on doing dirty, depraved filthy things to your body that has you coming back for more. It really could go either way when he smiles like that.

I'm hoping for the second option as I walk over to his side and he wraps his arm around my shoulders while staring down at me. I could drown in his eyes, so blue that it's like staring into the clearest part of the sea. But I won't forget that water is infested with sharks and I've caught the eye of the deadliest one.

"Yes?" I bite my lip, inching closer the longer he stares down at me with his head tilted.

I. Am. Drowning.

"Open up for me," he whispers in a throaty, dark voice and I obey without thinking as he places his fingers into my mouth while holding my gaze.

The first taste surprises me but I'm not unfamiliar with the coppery flavor of blood as my lips close around his index and middle digits. The salty, smooth texture that joins the first has my eyes fluttering closed as I moan around his fingers. I grab his wrist when he starts to pull away and swirl my tongue around him until there's nothing left to clean off of him. My eyes snap open when I hear a muttered curse in

Japanese and glance out of the corner of my eye to see Nicky leaning over the hood of his car with his arms crossed. His gaze latches onto my mouth and I suddenly feel like I have two predators within reaching distance that are dying to take a bite out of me. I slowly back away from Tey, wiping off the remaining flavor spread over my top lip with my thumb and lick the rest off with a small moan of bliss.

"You like that Peaches?" Tey questions as his fingers slide through my hair on the back of my nape.

A shiver cascades down my spine as I lean back into his touch, seeking more. It takes a great effort to keep my eyes open as he continues to play with my hair. The fucker knows it's every girl's weakness. I will say it's pretty comfortable and relaxing that it distracts my mind from what's to come.

"Delicious." My voice comes out raspy and deeper than normal.

How do they do that? Flip the switch in me from being freaked out, anxiety riding me high, to making me feel needy with damp panties?

"Hear that, Nicky? She likes the taste of us both mixed together." He winks at me and starts to steer me towards the door of the club. "He made such a sticky mess in the car and I knew you would help with that pretty mouth of yours. I love seeing my blood smeared across these pouty lips."

Before I can respond, my head is being turned by fingers grasping my jaw. Nicky's lips descend on mine in a rush that makes me dizzy. A good kind of dizziness that has your world spinning and you can only focus on one thing until everything just stops.

Hungry. Demanding. Feral.

That's how I would explain Nicky's lips devouring mine. Almost punishing but he takes his time moving his lips against mine, like he's sucking my soul out with each glide of his tongue sweeping into my mouth.

Just as quickly as it came, he stops just as fast and walks away like he didn't just rock my world with the heat of his sculpted lips.

"Sweetheart, I need you to do me a favor." Tey squeezes my shoulders and steers me through the club door. "I need you to prepare that sweet pussy for us because when the time comes we are going to stretch you so wide... at the same time."

My mouth goes dry. That sounds painful but my imagination is running wild and I like the thought of feeling both of them moving inside me, stretching me past my limit until it hurts. It's sick but I need to feel the pain to the point that my eyes water. I never wanted it before but since meeting the guys I know I'll be closer to heaven than I've ever been, my body dripping with pleasure. Needing the space, I step away from Tey as the door slams shut behind us and I take that moment to glance around Diablo.

Dalton lets out a low whistle and heads towards the long, gleaming, black bar across the dance floor. Suddenly bright lights flicker on from crystals hanging from the ceiling like curtains. My jaw practically drops open at how classy and sophisticated Dom's club is. I was kind of expecting a hole in the wall by the appearance from outside. The inside has three levels when I glance up, with red velvet couches on each level, and balconies looking down on the glowing dance floor.

"I didn't know you owned Diablo." Logan leans on the bar next to Dalton, his honey eyes tracking Dom as he goes behind the bar.

"I know you didn't. The great Logan Russo wouldn't dare set foot in my club if he would have known. I've watched you on my cameras a few times." Dom raises a brow at Lo as if he's daring him to start talking shit and sends a wink at me as he lines up shot glasses while pulling out a bottle of tequila.

"Little bitch, come over here and take a shot with us." Dalton grabs the loops of my jeans and pulls me under his arm while Dom holds out a glass to me.

The guys follow my example as Dom pours each of them a shot like a pro. Tey hops onto the counter as I raise my glass to my mouth and pulls his knife out to twirl between his fingers without reaching for a drink. He notices me staring and answers my unspoken question with a shrug.

"Been through too many foster homes with alcoholics." He watches me as I start to put the glass down and reaches around Nicky to place his fingers under my shot, making me throw it back in one swallow.

My throat fucking burns but I grew up on this shit around the compound and it goes down smoothly.

"Remind me to never challenge you in a drinking game," Dalton mutters in awe as he watches me, his voice gravelly as he slams his own shot glass down.

"Burns like a bitch but keeps the demons away." Dom salutes us and tosses his back like it's water.

"I've been drinking since I was twelve years old. You have to get tolerance starting at a young age when you live with a bunch of criminals." I laugh hollowly, sliding my glass to Dom for another.

The guys stay quiet, watching me shoot back two more shots before Dom nods his head for us to follow him. He starts climbing the stairs and Tey scoops me up, surprising me as he sprints up the steps after Dom.

We walk into a big office that overlooks the club down below with floor-to-ceiling, tinted windows. Tey spots the long sectional and sits down with me in his lap, turning me so I can lean my back against his chest. Dom walks towards his desk and leans back in his chair, watching me with his dark gaze that sees everything. Logan shuts the door and crosses his arms as he glances around, stopping on Dom with a glare, almost like he can't help himself. Nicky sits on one side of Tey, crossing his ankle over his leg as Dalton sits on the other side of me on the couch and kicks his boots up onto the coffee table.

"Right. Okay. We are doing this," I say, a warm buzz spreading through my body from the alcohol and making me sink further against Tey's.

"How about you start with why the hell you were dancing naked for other men?" Logan asks in a tight voice, his chest expanding as he takes a deep breath like he's trying to calm himself.

"I wasn't naked completely. I just wanted... No, that's not it. I *needed* to dance. You won't understand." I look away from Logan, glancing at the windows just as music starts thumping downstairs and strobe lights flash from each corner of the club.

"Then make us understand, Angel." Tey squeezes me around my waist, his voice quiet like he's almost scared that I'm going to shut down.

I just might.

"You guys understand what it's like growing up around powerful men. Men that get off on power and aren't afraid to use that against their own sons. But you don't know what it's like being a girl in a man's world." My throat goes dry and I avoid their gazes until Nicky speaks up next to me.

"I know more than you think. My father treats my sister like she is dysfunctional, a waste of space. Don't think the masks we wear every day mean we don't have our own battles going on behind closed doors. You know what Jin deals with in the human flesh trade." Nicky lets me in, and when I finally have the courage to glance over at him, I see past the sharp edges of his beautiful face. Everything is raw, bared out in the open for me to see. His mask of cool indifference is gone, but only for enough time for me to see how much hurt and fury he's hiding before his eyes harden, shutting me out once again. He hates this life too.

"I think I'm just starting to get that," I tell him, reaching over to slide my index finger down his smooth jawline.

"Tillie... I need you to tell me why. My every waking moment is filled with you and the dreams I have of you in the kitchen with Payne. Everything he said... was it true?" Dalton stares down at the club as it starts to fill up and his reflection in the mirror is one of rage, as if all his muscles are made of marble.

"Yes. I–I don't want you to look at me like I'm weak or pity me. This is my life and I've lived it every day, still waking up and getting out of bed. If you can't handle my past and what's happened, say it now." I clench my fists in my lap, hating the thought of anyone looking at me like I need to be sheltered, locked away because I've seen too much bad to last a lifetime.

"The moment I saw the fire spark in your eyes, standing up to Logan without a hint of fear... I knew I'd have to make you my Queen. Not someone to stand behind me, head bowed, but a woman that bathes in the blood of her enemies with a smile while standing by my side. That's you, mama." Dom stares at me with admiration in his gaze, his words hitting me deeply.

That's how he really sees me.

Strong.

Capable of killing anyone who hurts me.

I think I sink further into the trap Dom lured me into like a spider does for its prey at his words. I'm not trying to escape though. I want to stay tangled up in his webs.

"Smooth, you fucker," Dalton deadpans but a smirk plays on his lips.

Maybe I can bring all these guys together... I could be the glue and finally have a real family.

"You know what you look like to us, Tillie?" Logan actually uses my name, telling me he wants my attention.

"What?" I try to hide the shakiness in my voice, meeting his gaze head-on.

Whatever he says, I can take it.

"Ours."

That simple word. One small fucking word has my bottom lip trembling until I bite it to stop the sob that wants to climb up my throat.

"None of that. It's too tempting." Nicky releases my lip with his thumb while Tey places his head on my shoulder with a content sigh.

I'm surrounded by men that are dark, scary, and can snap a man's neck without a second thought but fuck if they can't make me melt with just a few words and looks.

They shake me right to my very core. I'll take every harsh word, kneel under a command but when I stand back up... I'm really treated like a queen.

I meet Dom's gaze, so knowing and dark. He gives me a small nod, telling me with the gesture that it's going to be okay.

"The day Rig disappeared was like losing a piece of myself and I didn't know how much of that was true until today. I think I always knew deep down... He protected me from the world as much as he could in our situation. Turns out he's actually my dad." I laugh at that last part, a tear dripping down my cheek until I quickly wipe it away.

"Diana?" Logan states, not looking away as I nod my head to confirm his suspicion. "Say the word, baby girl, and she disappears."

"No. I–I can't blame her for wanting to get away from the club, starting over. I can wish for different things, a relationship with her but I just can't. I wouldn't wish the life I've lived on my worst enemy." I take a deep breath, looking down as Nicky places his hand over my clenched fists.

"I'll keep looking for him, Tillie. We will get answers to where Rig disappeared to," Nicky promises and I believe him. He won't stop until he gets all the information.

It's just the kind of guy he is, knowledge is power for him. It's who he is and how he works, digging up all the secrets of others.

"I'm scared of where that's going to lead me. It's all going to come back to the one person I can never run from," I admit to myself, knowing in my gut that the person who stars in my nightmares had something to do with Rig leaving.

"Who?" Dom asks calmly but the small twitch of his left eye gives him away... he's boiling under that thick skin of his.

"He's a member of the Demon Jokers. I've been his obsession since the moment Payne took him under his wing. I just didn't see how much of a psychopath he was until it was too late." I feel my chest tighten, realizing this is it, and I'm not backing down from sharing my secrets.

The guys don't move or speak, probably seeing I need a second to gather myself. I take a deep breath before speaking once more. No more hiding.

"The day I turned sixteen Payne tortured me in the basement of the club. It wasn't anything new. Looking back on it, Rig really was protecting me but I think Payne finally realized I was never his kid. The moment Rig wasn't around, Payne started teaching me a lesson on obedience. Those were times that I wished I could run away. Every hit, every time he cut me... It wasn't until he called the club members into the room that I screamed for death. Each male in that room watched me grow up and they were the ones that took my last bit of innocence away." My voice comes out empty, numb as I gaze at the guys but not really seeing them.

I hear ragged breathing and look at Dalton across the

office to see his chest heaving like he just ran a marathon. His eyes are red as they water and he blinks harshly, shaking his head rapidly while rubbing at his chest.

"I was raped on the cold floor in the basement by each club member of Payne's inner circle. They also saved the worst of them for last." I sink further into Tey's rigid body, almost wanting to crawl in his skin and hide while feeling suddenly so tired.

"The scars?" Logan rasps out, pushing away from the door and falling to his knees by my feet as his hand hovers over the jagged lines on my flesh, the raised bumps each telling a story of my suffering.

"Those were all part of Payne's torture sessions." I feel the initial on my shoulder like a burn, asking for attention.

"What's this mean?" Tey asks, tracing the bump of the letter C through my shirt.

"A reminder," I say, holding on tight to Nicky's hand and drawing courage from him when he squeezes back.

"For what?" Dom suddenly stands up, his chair knocking over as he leans his hands across the desk.

"Ownership." I inhale sharply as Tey tightens his grip around my waist, almost to the point of pain and Dalton lets out an outraged shout.

I watch as he paces like a wild animal before punching the glass window. His knuckles split open and leave smears of blood behind on the glass.

"Let me up," I choke out, tapping Tey's forearm and slowly climbing to my feet as he reluctantly lets me go while I step around Logan as he stays kneeling in place without saying a word.

I walk over on quiet feet to Dalton and hesitantly place my hand on his back. His body shudders at my touch and he stops hitting the glass, dropping his head against the window with his shoulders hunched.

"I thought he was just trying to taunt me. Bound and gagged, feeling helpless. I'll never forgive myself, Tillie, for not being able to do anything as Payne touched you," Dalton whispers, almost like he's confessing his sins to a priest.

"There isn't anything to forgive. I lived through it and am still standing." I've never spoken truer words, I'm a survivor.

"We need a name, baby girl." Logan's voice drifts over to me, so much anger in the quiet way he demands.

"It doesn't matter anymore." I shake my head and jump as I'm suddenly spun around by my arms, looking up at a very pissed off Logan.

I didn't even hear him move.

"Doesn't matter?" he questions, his eyes flickering back and forth between mine, as if he's looking for something.

"I was raped, Logan. I'm already damaged. There's nothing you can do about it." I shrug under his tight hold and watch as he looks over his shoulder with a nod.

"On your knees." Logan's voice changes, going deeper with a sharp command.

"Wh–what?" I stutter, not knowing what game he is playing.

"You heard him." Tey appears at his side, twirling his knife between his fingers.

I glance over my shoulder up at Dalton, expecting him to stick up for me but all I get is a blank expression in return.

"Don't make him repeat himself, Tillie. You won't like the outcome," Nicky casually says, sliding into place by Logan's other side.

The day in the garage comes back to me, it's where I knew I'd never have the physical strength to fight them back. I still have my sanity and my own mind at least. I thought Dom would step in at some point to stop this but when I glance over at him he's back in his chair and watching like a king on his throne.

Seeing every single one of them dead serious I slowly sink to my knees while glaring with my head tilted all the way back so I can see them as they circle around me like kings standing over their subjects.

Fingers glide along my nape before sinking into my hair and sliding up while pulling until my head is bent back.

"What do you feel at this very moment?" Nicky asks as he strokes a finger down my cheek, caressing my jaw until his thumb stops at the indent of the middle of my lips.

What do I feel right this second?

Anger.

Grief.

... Alive.

I don't want to think of the past, living in it constantly, of what I had to go through to survive. I want this moment, right now, with desire coursing through me, making me feel light-headed and knowing only these five, cruel men can make my heart race at a wild speed that's almost unhealthy.

"Everything," I reply back, feeling the plush carpet cushioning my knees and my chest expanding with each deep breath.

"Do you know what I see from this height?" Tey leans down, his hand snapping forward and closing around my throat with the right amount of pressure to make me feel like I'm floating but grounded at the same time.

"Power," Dalton answers for him, the hand in my hair pulling harder, making my eyes practically roll to the back of my head with intense pleasure.

"You see, Tillie, it's not those who force someone onto their knees with all the power. It's the person who kneels down, plots their deaths, and still rise to keep fighting. You have us wrapped around your fingers and don't even realize it." Logan's voice is soft yet deep, holding my attention so that every word out of his beautiful mouth holds my absolute attention.

"The question is, mama, do you want this? What you see is what you get." Dom's Hispanic accent seeps through his words, soaking into my skin like a warm bath.

Blinking once, I gaze at the men surrounding me, dominating and turning me into a submissive that I would happily do anything for them. I thought I would always despise letting a man control me. But here I am. On my knees, begging practically for their touch. I'm beginning to realize the difference between ownership Cruz demanded without leaving me a choice. I want to be there, I want to be their property. Treat me like a woman, make me beg in the bedroom, and take care of me after. I was treated like an outsider in the beginning, the first moment I met Logan he mistrusted me but eventually saw the real me, past all the scars and tattoos. These guys cracked me wide up and have slowly been picking up the pieces to right a wrong they caused. I'm going to keep them, that's my decision.

My property.

"Yes," I answer in a breathy tone.

Tey adds more pressure on my throat before leaning forward to place his nose against my neck, inhaling loudly and letting out a moan. Dalton pets my hair, stroking his fingers through the curls and making me purr. Feels so fucking good. Nicky presses his thumb harder against my lips, making me realize he's been feeling my lips for any lies that might slip through and finds them lacking.

I'm a hundred percent in, there isn't any turning back.

"Good girl. Say it," Logan suddenly demands in a voice like dark chocolate, staring down at my upturned face with a raised eyebrow.

"Your slut," I rasp, leaning into their touches, almost desperate for attention.

I can feel how pleased the guys are, the room tense with our pent-up desire and it's about to snap any second. I need this, it's a better feeling than dancing. I'd rather be trapped in their grasp, saturated in pleasure, and be protected in strong arms that won't let anything harm me.

Maybe I've always been cut out for this life.

If they're the bad guys then I'll just have to become very, very bad in return.

"My Queen," Dom practically purrs with that slight accent of his, causing goosebumps to cover every inch of my skin.

"My old lady." Dalton grips my hair and tugs on the curls, bringing my head flush against his strong thighs.

"My beautiful, psycho killer." I would laugh at Tey for the cute nickname but his voice sounds affectionate and happy while slightly unhinged.

Wouldn't have him any other way.

"Ours." Nicky, so quiet but his voice so deep that it vibrates in my ear with the truth.

This is it. Honest and open finally between each other. I'm not looked at with disgust but desire so hot that anyone looking at us would be caught on fire.

"I'm yours, my body and soul, and you're all mine." Heat curls in my stomach at the tension thick in the air, and a small shudder runs through my body that I can almost taste their dark desires.

"You trust us?" Nicky asks, undoing his tie around his neck while never looking away from me.

"Not one bit," I say cheekily, feeling light and fucking free.

"That's our girl." Logan reaches for my hand and puts it over the hard length straining his pants, squeezing his fist around our clasped fingers until I can feel every single hard inch of his cock. "No one else can do this for me. Have me coming back for more, needing their touch so badly that I feel like I'm going crazy. I need you, Tillie."

I swear he just cracked my chest wide open and pulled my pulsing heart out into the palm of his hands.

"Real smooth, Romeo. Who knew you were a fucking poet?" Tey says to Logan before gazing back at me with a smirk, his tongue licking over his bottom lip as he stares at me. "No peeking, Peaches. Let us worship you."

I should be scared but fuck if my pussy doesn't flutter at his words.

The silk tie Nicky untied from his neck is placed over my eyes, blocking my view. Everything is heightened now. All I can hear is my own breathing, and my skin tingles with awareness. A hand slides down my arm, making me jump at the contact.

"So sensitive," Nicky whispers, the heat of his words against my earlobe before he moves away.

I'm suddenly lifted into strong arms, cradled in a hold with one hand palming my ass and the other under my shoulders. My lips twitch knowing that Dalton is carrying me. No one has big biceps like him, I could cuddle into those bad boys forever.

He places me on my feet, not saying anything as he steps away so quietly I can't place where he went. A pair of smooth, plump lips glide over the pounding pulse of my neck, making me tilt my head back on a moan. Open-mouthed kisses are placed on the other side of my neck and I have to reach out to hold onto the edge of the desk as my ass makes contact with the surface of the hardwood as my knees wobble.

My lips part, moans spilling out as I feel every little touch. My nipples pebble almost painfully as a big hand grips my left breast, massaging me and pinching my nipples into hard pebbles. I let out a whimper and bite my bottom lip, trying to hold in the needy sound.

"Don't hold back those beautiful noises. Shirt off, baby girl," Logan growls out in front of me and I lift my arms up as my shirt is pulled over my head.

Just when I'm about to lower my arms back down, I'm stopped when one of them wraps around both of my wrists in one palm from behind as calloused hands return to my breasts gripping and tugging at my sensitive nipples.

"Lower her over my desk," Dom's sexy voice is thick with lust and deep, the grip on my wrist squeezing lightly.

"Don't fucking order me around," Logan grinds out as I'm lifted into the air again and placed in the middle of Dom's desk.

There's a gentle tug on my wrist and I lower back until my whole upper body is draped over his desk and I'm on display.

"Fuck you too, Russo," Dom replies back in rapid Spanish and I can't help the grin that comes over my face at the light banter between them.

They sound like two kids fighting over a toy.

"You find something funny, baby girl?" Logan asks with a smile in his voice.

My grin melts off my lips as the mouths that followed me down on the desk move away and the hand switching back and forth between my breasts is missing too. I'm full-on frowning now, the bliss I was feeling being taken away too suddenly has my body feeling like a hot fuse about to explode.

"What happened to being worshiped?" I sass back and take a deep breath to calm my racing heart.

"Damn. That mouth is sure to get you into trouble, Killer," Tey mutters with a chuckle.

"Maybe I want to get into trouble." I'm trying really hard to not pout, needing someone to fucking touch me already.

My pussy is dripping wet, soaking through my panties and I'm dying to be claimed.

"How about we give these luscious lips something else to do besides being a mouthy brat?" Dalton suggests, his voice gravelly and hot.

Oh fuck.

"Lift your ass for me," Nicky's tone is deliciously authoritative and dark, It's always the quiet ones that like ass play.

My breathing is too loud but I swear every time they speak... I feel their voices travel straight to my pussy and it makes me shiver in desire. I follow his directions as his fingers flick my jeans open and drag them slowly down my legs. I'm scooted back on the desk until my head is leaning over the edge, making me slightly dizzy as the blood rushes to my head.

"I look at you and still can't believe you're real. Absolutely perfect." Dom's Spanish is flawless and beautiful coming from his mouth.

I feel like a flower blooming under his words, spreading my legs under their watchful gazes. I want to be devoured by them.

Fingers slide up my outer thighs and grasp my panties, taking their time dragging them down my legs. I can feel my juices coat my inner thighs and slide down until it's leaving a puddle under me on Dom's desk.

No one says a word but the sudden trails of lips on my thighs have my back arching and me panting when I realize I have two mouths trailing up my legs on both sides, heading right for my greedy pussy. My bound hands are freed as I shift around and I lower them from above my head until two sets of hands pin my hands flat down on either side of the desk so I can't move.

"Try not to move, mama, open wide and relax your throat," Dom warns before the velvety head of his cock glides across my bottom lip and I open my mouth without hesitation.

I've never been a fan of sucking off a guy but these guys make me feel like I'm dying, starving for their cum to coat my throat.

The angle is different. For some reason I can feel him more, his cock taking up my whole mouth and stretching my jaw until it aches. He slides down my throat, massaging my exposed neck with his fingers and feeling his cock block my airway. He can probably see his cock slipping down, moving in and out at an unhurried pace.

"That's a good fucking girl," Dom praises me with a growl, holding still as I breathe through my nose at the upside down angle.

Saliva and tears run down my cheeks as I gag around him, my hands flexing to grasp something as I breathe through my nose. A bite on my left inner thigh causes me to jerk at the sting before he lathers his tongue smoothly over the throbbing pain as if to take away the pain. I can't stop moving restlessly as the mouth on my right thigh licks past the spot I need him the most and he continues to leave nipping bites on my hip bone with a dark chuckle. The cold, metal ball on his tongue tells me it's Tey teasing me, and the only other man who has enough self-control to torture me until I'm ready to combust has to be Nicky.

Both men on either side of my thighs hold me wide open, leaving open-mouth kisses and their hot breath hovering right over my dripping hole. I double my efforts on sucking Dom deeper, humming in pleasure as he groans and clasps his fingers around my neck to feel him moving inside. Fingers lightly part my lower lips, and I can feel them staring at my pussy, seeing the dripping mess pooling, how on edge I am to feel their tongues right on my clit.

"Shame I didn't save your cum to shove up in this pretty, pink pussy," Tey mumbles, sounding distracted but I couldn't focus even if I tried.

Both tongues attack my pussy at the same time, lapping like starving men on a mission to destroy me. I'm a sloppy mess, hearing the wet slurping that goes in perfect sync each time I choke on Dom. My head pounds, limbs shaking but I don't ask them to stop.

I can feel Tey and Nicky sliding the flat of their tongues on either side of my pussy lips, heading towards my entrance with long, teasing strokes. My mind runs wild. I can picture them clearly, mouths moving together, touching. The thought of them making out, eating my pussy at the same time heightens my pleasure that my legs start to shake violently.

"Someone likes that. Keep doing that. She's going to come." Dalton's husky voice sounds from my right, and I'm unbelievably sopping wet knowing he's watching my body be destroyed in the best way.

I almost feel bad about putting him on a sex ban but at this second I don't give a shit. Lights dance behind my mask, and Dom is as deep as he can go down my throat, making it difficult to breathe. Without warning two fingers slip inside my pussy and hook right on my G-spot with a gentle rub on my walls as Tey's tongue piercing flickers in rapid succession over my clit before sucking.

Pressure so intense balls up in my stomach as colorful stars burst across my closed eyes, my whole body going taut as I start to come. I moan loudly around Dom, and he quickly slips out of my mouth just as I scream in pleasure. Wetness gushes from between my legs and gathers under me on the desk, making it slippery as I tremble in place.

"Fucking hell. I love it when she squirts," Tey groans out before lapping at the juices still leaking out of my pussy, and humming in pleasure as I fill his mouth.

"You're perfect, mama," Dom pants from above me,

massaging my neck and shoulders as he no doubt watches the show.

The feeling of teeth piercing my inner thigh hard enough that I can feel blood gliding towards my hip bone causes me to whimper just as he licks the spot tenderly. I know Nicky probably left another scar on my leg but I'm not mad about it. I'm surprised it wasn't Tey with his obsession with blood, then again he said he'll wait until I'm bleeding... the kinky fucker. My periods are so irregular from my birth control that it might be a while before he gets his wish.

The silk tie unwinds and is pulled off, leaving me blinking rapidly up at Dom's dark eyes staring down at me with admiration. Arms wrapping around under my ass and pulling me closer to the desk edge has me looking down my body to see Logan standing between my spread legs with a glare aimed at Dom.

"I'm not sharing her with you at the same time. You can just fuck off." Logan's eyes narrow, the light honey color darkening with his anger as he has a stare off with Dom.

"Over my dead body. Homie, you're in my territory. So how about you fuck off?" Dom replies back, pissed off.

I hold my breath, hating that there's this gap of hatred between them that stems back to their childhood of violence that they had nothing to do with but that's not going to change overnight. It's actually a miracle one of them hasn't pulled a gun on the other yet.

Faster than I can blink, Dom is pointing a Glock at Logan. Well, there goes that thought. Everyone tenses and the air changes with static electricity just before a storm hits. I'm not letting this one good thing in my life slip through my fingers. I'll go to the extreme to make sure they don't murder each other.

I eye both of them, noticing not one of them is glancing at me except Tey who is sinking back into the couch with a smirk before winking at me. Dalton and Nicky follow Tey's example, joining him to watch the shitshow unfold. Guess it's in my hands to fix this.

I shoot up quickly into a sitting position and grasp Logan's thick cock to shut him up while I'm getting off on the control I have over him.

"I'll fucking kill you before you can pull that trigge—" I cut off any reply he was about to say to Dom as I line him up with my pussy and before he can stop me, I inch his big, thick cock inside me.

A sigh of bliss escapes my parted lips as I sink onto him with a roll of my hips. I love how he can't contain his groan of pleasure, his big hands grasping my hips. I lay flat on my back as he pumps into me, arching my back while reaching behind me for Dom's wrist. He lets me guide his hand, watching Logan's cock sliding in and out of me as if mesmerized. I point his gun towards my head at my temple and shift until my head is hanging over the edge of the desk again.

Swirling my tongue around Dom's cock, he inches back and stares at me as if he's trying to figure me out. The click of the safety coming off his gun makes my heart race but it doesn't stop the words spilling out of my mouth.

"More. Please," I beg, wrapping my legs around Logan's hips until I'm pressing the heels of my feet against his lower back to urge him to go faster.

Dom watches with that predatory gaze of his, not missing a thing and he lovingly strokes the edge of his gun down my face as my vision becomes fuzzy with the feeling of pleasure running through my veins. I reach for him, grabbing the front of his pants with a whimper of need and letting out a sigh as he steps forward without denying me what I crave. My mouth stretches, already aching around his girth but that doesn't stop me from sliding my tongue down his cock as I swallow him to the back of my throat.

"Someone just kill me, please. This is the worst torture, my balls are so blue." Dalton moans like he's dying, making me feel bad but this is about me for once.

My chest heaves, feeling like the life is being choked out of me by Dom's cock as I gag around him before remembering to breathe through my nose. Logan grasps my hips, lifting until my ass is off the desk and back arched. The new angle makes my pussy clench tighter around him, fluttering as an orgasm comes closer and closer. I just need a push to fall over straight into euphoria.

"You need more don't you, baby girl?" Logan states, his voice threatening. "Time for your punishment."

I can't respond, but hum around Dom as he roughly fucks my mouth, picking up speed. But I for sure feel the punishment Logan decides to use on me as he wraps an arm behind my lower back and rubs his other hand over my aching pussy, squeezing the flesh between his fingers before his touch disappears. The first slap has me whimpering, surprised that he literally just smacked my pussy, right over my clit.

"Oh fuck yeah. Punish her!" Tey cheers him on by the couch, clapping as Logan slaps me again and again.

I could tell myself that I don't like what he's doing, how it hurts, but my body would betray my lies. His cock slides in and out faster, matching Dom's rough pace to my mouth and there's no mistaking the wet sounds coming from me how much I love this. Gagging, drool slipping from my mouth, and the wet smack Logan lands on my pussy each time echoes around the room.

Dom wraps his fingers under my jaw, pulling my head farther back and completely cutting off my oxygen. His gun digs into the side of my head harder, making it more real that a loaded gun is pointing right at me. It could go off any second.

That thought and Logan sending one more hard smack

over my clit with the flat of his palm has my body convulsing on the table. The orgasm destroys me. I gasp for air, feeling like I'm faint but also floating in ecstasy. My hips can't stop jerking in his grasp as he pulls out of me to watch me squirt again before he's ramming back inside my pussy once more. I vaguely hear him as I float down from that intense orgasm. He lets out a sharp hiss between his teeth as rope after rope of cum coats my insides.

"Swallow it all down, mama," Dom grunts out, warning me just as he slides into the back of my throat one more time.

I can feel his cock pulse on my tongue, his salty, musky cum shooting down my throat until I swallow every last drop greedily. He pulls out of my mouth, his chest heaving as he helps me sit up. My jaw and shoulder hurt from the rough angle of hanging upside down, and an ache pulses with my heartbeat on my pussy where I can see how red it is from Logan smacking me.

"Dance half naked in front of men who are not us again, and your punishment will be much worse," Logan says darkly as he gently moves my sweaty hair off my forehead as I sit there panting for breath.

"Maybe... Maybe I should piss you off more, dearest stepbrother," I rasp out, my throat sore but in a good way.

"I'm sure I'll have plenty of time in the near future to schedule you in for another punishment, spoiled stepsister," Logan teases, a dimple forming in his cheek that hardly ever makes an appearance but makes me melt all the same.

I love it when he smiles. He looks more carefree and not like he has the weight of the world on his shoulders.

"Don't worry. I still have to deliver my punishment," Nicky says quietly and I turn my head towards him, gulping as I see the dark promise in his glittering, dark green eyes.

"We need a name, Tillie," Dom mutters from behind me,

pulling my arms up as he slips my shirt over my head before placing a sweet kiss on my temple where he held his gun.

"Cruz." I heave a breath, feeling a weight settle in my stomach as I push Logan back a step, and grab my pants off the floor once I slip off the desk on wobbly legs.

Cum leaks down my thighs, soaking into my skin and it takes everything inside of me to not spread it on my body to drive the guys nuts. I focus on the sticky mess coating me instead of looking into anyone's eyes. I pull my pants up, stalling as the zipper echoes in the room, and almost jump out of my skin when a finger gently lifts my head by the jaw.

"He's a dead man. I swear he won't ever hurt you again." Tey stares down into my face, murder blazing in his gaze as he makes me fall harder for him with just that promise alone.

"Let's go get some more tequila, get a little drunk, and regret it in the morning just before we have to head to school." Dalton grabs my hand, lifting it to kiss my palm with a slight smile curling his lips.

I really read him wrong the first time we met. The rough biker with a teacher sucking him off was all for show. So hard around the edges but deep inside he's just a gentle giant looking for cuddles and of course pussy but still.

"I'm not ready to go back to the house yet so let's go get our drunk on." I meet Logan's gaze as his fingers slide lovingly through my hair, untangling the wild, sex strands, nodding his head in agreement.

You know what? Fuck Diana and Franco. Everyone else can go to hell too. It's just me and my guys against the world.

CHAPTER 12

Franco

"What ages are coming in the shipment?" I put Jin on speaker, checking my computer for the numbers of supplies coming in and guests attending next weekend.

"Twelve and up. Better for grooming at a young age. We have very eager buyers this round. The turnout will be good," Jin mutters distractedly before barking out orders in rapid Japanese. He better be talking to someone else and not me.

"Good, good," I reply back, seeing the bidding prices.

The path I'm going down will make me the most powerful man in the state, and money falling into my lap the higher I climb in politics. Running for mayor will just be the extra bonus until I have everyone in my pocket. This city will pay for taking away the one thing I loved on this earth.

"I've heard that our boys were spotted with the blonde girl out in public. The annoying one with the high-pitched voice. It would seem they aren't as invested in their new pet, doesn't it? I've told Nicky to bring his pet to the auction. I figured she can earn her place by dancing until I decide to put her up for sale." Jin hums in amusement, probably already calculating the type of money he can make by putting her up on the auction block.

"Oh, the Paris girl. Her father is a judge, she has potential. Useful in the future. I'll order Logan to bring her to dinner soon," I mutter distractedly, wondering what game Logan is playing.

If my boy thinks I'll fall for that, trying to get my attention off his plaything... he really doesn't know me then. I've tasted that young pussy, so youthful and her smooth skin... It was an aphrodisiac, tasting her, and not a hardship. Payne didn't have to command me to eat her out, I would have done so willingly. He just gave me a reason to do it sooner rather than later.

What is so special about this girl that has Logan tied up in knots? She has that air of confidence about her that my Helen had but my son needs to learn that women will make him weak. They are only made for one thing and that's getting their hole fucked. If he thinks he's in love, I'll prove my point that it doesn't exist by pounding into Tillie's cunt next time in front of him. I really should just get rid of her before she corrupts my son and ruins my plans.

"Excellent idea. I have to go, a new supply of cocaine just came in. Make sure your boys in blue stay away from the warehouse. I'll be taste testing for the rest of the day." Jin hangs up without waiting for a reply.

I wonder sometimes where I'd be right now if he never took me under his wing, handing over a part of his empire to me until I could expand my business of counterfeit money and drugs. I'd probably be a detective behind a desk, drowning in alcohol, or in jail for getting caught murdering Dom's father. I never thought I'd be here, involving myself in the trade business but when Jin asked, I couldn't refuse. He saved me, I owed him and he has a shipment coming in from across seas that will make him millions. I don't trust him but then again I trust no one. I just recently got involved in the flesh trade and when the time is right, I'll take his whole empire away from him. Jin doesn't deserve it because I still view him as a criminal that helped get my wife killed, with drugs that I thought I could get off the streets as a rookie cop. I was a fool but never again. I will be the only one who distributes anything in and out of this state, watching as other families fall apart so they can feel the pain of losing a loved one.

"Hold on, baby girl. Let me carry you up the stairs." My son's voice echoes down the hallway and I push away from my desk to see what's happening as a thump sounds near the front of the house.

Silently striding down the hall, I turn the corner just as he bends down to carry Tillie upstairs. Her one shoe is sitting at the bottom of the foyer, left behind, and her drunk mumbling drifts down to me from the top of the staircase. I raise a brow and follow behind them, curious as to why my boy is being so gentle with her. He barely stares at her when I'm around, acting like she's a disease that he could catch. He's been putting on a very convincing show for me since she showed up at my house in the middle of the night. Stopping at Tillie's doorway, I stay behind in the shadows as I peek between the crack of her door.

"Lo, can you stay with me tonight? I don't want to be alone." Tillie grasps his hand as he starts to turn away after tucking her in, pulling off her other shoe.

"I'm not going anywhere. I'm just going to go take a quick shower and I'll be right back," he replies, leaning down to whisper something in her ear that has a goofy smile curling her lips, and walks away into the bathroom.

I wait in the doorway until I hear the shower turn on and step into the room. Tillie tosses and turns before settling on her side facing me, her arm hanging over the side of the bed and the sheets pooling at her waist. I approach on quiet feet, waiting to see if she can recognize me but she just blinks sleepily at me with a drunk, lopsided grin spreading across her plump lips. A little bit too drunk on a school night but it comes to my advantage. She'll pass out soon enough. Slowly lowering onto the corner of her bed, I brush her hair off her forehead and arch a brow as she nuzzles her face into my hand.

"Logan." She sighs dreamily with a smile before drifting off to sleep.

This won't do at all. She has my son wrapped around her finger just like his mother had me wrapped around hers. He will only come out of this in pain of a broken heart. I thought I beat physical pain into him over the years with my belt so he's numb to everything else but this is different. She can warm his heart and rip it away at the same time. I need to deal with the problem before it's too late. It will be my final lesson for Logan, even his own blood will hurt him in the end. I told him time and time again to never trust anyone but he doesn't listen. After this auction, I'll make sure she disappears.

I could hand her back over the Demon Jokers. After the way Payne died and was delivered at their doorstep, they are without a doubt seeking revenge. I can lay the bread crumbs for the motorcycle gang that won't lead back to me, they won't be able to resist coming for Tillie. Or I can take her when she's alone and put a bullet through her head just like how my Helen was killed.

I trace her soft lips with my finger, feeling the heat of her breath, and wonder if I should fuck her to teach both her and Logan a lesson before killing her. Everything in this city is mine. The shower turns off and I slowly pull my hand away from the beautiful disaster, leaning forward to whisper in her ear before I leave her room.

"I did warn you. Mess with my family and I'll kill you."

Dalton

I didn't sleep last night. I couldn't. I was there when Payne and his fucking goons talked about raping Tillie but I didn't want to believe it. Hearing her yesterday at Dom's club... it makes me want to tear the world apart and kill everyone that's ever hurt her. I'm included in that... I can't even begin to wonder how she can stand the sight of me.

My thoughts have been all over the place. I already know I'm going to lead my club into a war but that was decided the night the Demon Jokers touched my little bitch.

"If you keep making that face, she's going to know what you're thinking." Nicky pats my shoulder as he claims the seat next to me and pulls out his lunch and a pair of chopsticks.

"I can't help it. I want to kill every fucker who hurt her, looked at her wrong. I just want to right my wrongs and protect her," I grumble out, sinking in my seat as I watch Tillie make her way across the outdoor courtyard with Logan and Tey.

"Suck it up, butter–buttercup. My bestie's a fighter, not a pussy," Nicola declares as she slams her tray on the table, her head ticking to the side as she sits down with Evan not far behind her. "Did Mom make you some octopus? The hell?! I swear that woman only shows her love when she's cooking."

I don't watch but I already know Nicola is trying to steal Nicky's lunch as he holds her away with the palm of his hand to her forehead without looking at her. It's nothing new, his little sister is a food thief.

"Little bitch." My voice comes out gravelly from lack of sleep last night.

I pat my leg as she approaches the table, noticing the sunglasses she has covering her eyes and how she walks slowly. I can't blame her. My balls feel like they're going to fall off after watching her come last night over and over. My cock hardens as if he knows she's near, begging to sink inside her heat.

"I missed you. Never knew I'd like sleeping next to someone," she whispers in my ear before sitting her luscious ass right over my hard cock and squirming like she enjoys torturing me.

The vixen.

"What am I? Chop liver?" Logan growls out, leaning back in his seat but looking relaxed as hell which is new.

"I will admit I did enjoy drooling all over you but your grumpy ass needs to chill in the morning. What kind of monster opens the blinds first thing when waking up?!" Tillie jokes, pushing her sunglasses up and reaching for some of Nicky's sushi.

My jaw drops when he doesn't bat her away but pushes the box closer to her without saying a word. He won't ever admit it but he's a food hoarder just like his sister.

"When am I going to be invited to the sleepover? I'm feeling left out." Tey pouts, twirling a lock of her hair around his finger as he gives her puppy eyes.

"Tonight? I've never been in a puppy pile before but if you keep giving me those puppy eyes then I'll be demanding it every night. Who knew you guys loved cuddles?" Tillie turns to face me, her expression teasing yet there are dark circles under her eyes so I can't tell if that's from the drinking last night or if she's mentally exhausted.

"Do you need anything?" I ask quietly, leaning forward to rub my beard into the crook of her neck and wrapping my arms around her waist as she squirms in my lap with a loud laugh.

"Mercy!" she cries out, trying to catch her breath as I ease up a little.

"Don't you know, toy? We are merciless," Nicky states matter-of-factly and he's not wrong.

"If you don't knock it off, I'll never dance for you," she threatens me and I instantly stop tickling her with my beard.

"Dalton, my brother from another mother, I'll cut off your balls, pan fry them, and then force-feed them to you if you tickle her one more time," Tey claims so calmly, his voice completely serious for once.

Tillie turns towards him with a soft smile and blows. His dramatic ass pretends to catch her kisses, almost falling out of his chair while flashing his knife as if he dares anyone to try to steal his air-kisses. Tillie has tears of laughter trailing down her cheeks as she watches him, shaking her head at his ridiculousness. Tey, instead of pretending to eat her kisses, pulls his jeans away from his stomach slightly, flashing a hint of his abs with a wink at her, and drops her kiss down his pants.

"I can not deal with you fuckers. Why are we friends again?" Logan deadpans, ignoring the sharp knife Tey is using to carve something into the table.

I swear nothing frazzles Logan. I won't admit this to the guys ever but I used to worry about Tey going unhinged and really losing it one day to the point of no return. I pictured seeing a bullet in his forehead, Logan's gun still smoking after having to put him down. Tillie... She sees all our dark sides but she brings out something I'd never seen in any of us. A gentle side of someone falling in love.

Hell. I've already fallen, fucking hard.

"I'd advise you to keep it down. You're disturbing the other students, this school isn't a zoo."

Fuck. Just fuck my life. My eyes squeeze shut at the voice directly behind me and I tighten my hold on Tillie like I'm afraid my touch is suddenly going to disgust her.

Everyone stops talking, and Tillie's laughter dies off when she realizes Mrs. Sullivan is behind me and addressing her.

"Of course. We wouldn't want to break any rules that affect the other students," Tillie replies back, her voice even and calm.

I open my eyes and see her smiling sweetly at Mrs. Sullivan like she never seen her sucking my cock. I glance around at the guys, confused as fuck as to why Tillie is being nice and not causing a bloodbath. All the guys are glaring behind me until I hear a ridiculous humph and a click of heels walking away. I blow out a relieved breath, making eye contact with Logan who slowly shakes his head like he knew exactly what I was thinking. Getting rid of Mrs. Sullivan would help a lot of things, mainly making Tillie's life easier since she has a class with her. But of course, Franco told us to stay out of the spotlight of the media and a missing teacher would do the opposite of that. My muscles strain, the tension thick in the air even after the sexual predator left.

"You know, I've never been to a slumber party. Can I come?" Evan announces, breaking the ice as we all turn to him with incredulous looks.

"The fuck you say?" Logan growls out, leaning threateningly in his seat.

"I don't know if I should invite you because that's sad as fuck or kill you now for even thinking of sleeping over at our girl's place." Tey chuckles, the dark type of chuckle that means he's serious and crazy.

"We can have our own sleepover instead. Banana. Eek," Nicola says innocently, throwing her banana peel over her shoulder with a jerk of her arm and reaching over to pet Evan's arm.

"The sun is shining. It seems like a good day to kill someone." Nicky's voice is deep, his intense stare never breaking eye contact with Evan.

Tillie doesn't say anything, she's lightly sliding her nails back and forth across the back of my neck. A quiet woman is never a good thing.

"I'll be right back. Going to the restroom." She kisses my cheek and stands from my lap, not making eye contact with anyone as she walks away.

"Fine! I'll never go to a sleepover!" Evan yells, his voice a higher pitch than before but I don't look away from Tillie as she walks into the building.

That's not the way towards the restrooms. I turn and see Tey sitting closer to Evan, dragging his knife loudly across the table. Nicky and Logan are staring at me then to the door she disappeared through. They think she's up to something too.

"I'll be right back." I get up, abandoning my lunch, and walk calmly after Tillie.

Once inside, I look around and see her climbing the stairs to the second floor down the hallway. She doesn't look at anyone as she passes students, shoving them aside without a backwards glance. My brows furrow in curiosity until it clicks where she's going.

Oh fuck.

I take off down the hall after her, dodging students until they move like the Red Sea and get out of my way. By the time I make it to the stairs, she has a good head start on me. Climbing them two at a time, I reach the top of the landing and immediately head towards Mrs. Sullivan's classroom at the end of the hallway. It's the teachers' lunch hour too so she'll be all alone in her classroom. Honestly, I'm curious what my little bitch will do. Tillie's already inside when I finally make it to the door of the classroom, I press my ear to the thick wood and hear two female voices but can't make out what's being said. Grabbing the door handle, I turn it slowly and slip through the gap big enough for my body to fit through. The door shuts quietly behind me so they don't know I'm here but my jaw hangs open at the sight before me of both their side profiles.

You know, I thought I'd either find Tillie crying or at least kicking the shit out of Mrs.Sullivan. I was completely wrong, so wrong.

"I can make you come better than any man has before. I can find your G-spot with my eyes closed, your pussy squeezing my fingers tightly as you come again and again." Tillie's voice changes into a seductive purr and I'm almost afraid to blink just in case I miss anything.

It's like looking at a different person. Her body language is more relaxed, the seductress standing in front of Mrs.Sullivan without touching her. She crowds her body, making sure her chocolate brown gaze is locked on Mrs.Sullivan.

"I–I–I'm not into women," Mrs.Sullivan stutters, taken by surprise but I can see her gaze travel down Tillie's body with lust darkening her eyes.

"Neither am I. There's just something I can't resist about you. Sexy as fuck." Tillie's eyes become hooded, stepping closer to Mrs.Sullivan until her breasts graze the front of the teacher's button-down, slutty blouse.

"It's not right," Mrs.Sullivan whispers but without conviction in her voice.

"I promise I won't say anything," Tillie says, crooking her hip until her thigh rests between Mrs. Sullivan's legs, the other fucking woman rolling her hips against my little bitch like she can't help herself.

I should be afraid of the creature of lust in front of me, but I'm not. I can't look away from her. Hell, I didn't even know she could be this deadly, her body screams seduction and lust. She's drawing her prey into her web without hardly having to try. She's amazing.

"Jus–Just this once." Mrs.Sullivan gives in so easily it's almost disgusting but you can't resist the spell Tillie casts.

I think I'm only beginning to see a side of Tillie she doesn't let out. I saw her kill Miguel in the warehouse but this is different. She only has to use her voice and her body to get what she wants. Fuck, she's dangerous and the most beautiful thing I've ever seen.

"Take off your clothes and sit in your desk chair with your legs spread," Tillie says in a raspy voice that goes straight to my cock.

I reach down and squeeze my dick to ease the pain without looking away from Tillie as she sways her hips while walking around the front of the desk, climbing on top, and spreading her legs wide open. Her skirt rides up to her hips, giving me a clear view of her silk, pink panties. I wish we were the only ones in here so I can slip into her tight pussy and never leave.

"You're beautiful." Mrs.Sullivan pants, her clothes shredded on the floor as she lowers herself into the chair in front of Tillie in just her bra and underwear.

"I know," Tillie says, leaning back on her arm and taking her time sliding the palm of her hand up her bare thigh teasingly, drawing Mrs. Sullivan's eyes right where she wants them.

My gaze is locked on her, only her, waiting to see how far she's going to take this and that's why I notice the barely there movement behind her as she lets out a fake as fuck moan.

While distracting Mrs.Sullivan, her fingers playing right over the edge of her panties, my girl reaches behind her with her other hand. She slowly winds up the mouse cord that's attached to the computer in her fist.

"Tell me how much you want this. How badly do you want to come?" Tillie gets in her face, ripping the cord from the computer and holding all of Mrs. Sullivan's attention by grasping her jaw before trailing one finger down until it rests between her fake boobs.

Tillie has better breasts, a handful, perky, and real as fuck.

My jaw grinds as I watch Tillie slide off the desk as smooth as butter, straddling our fucking teacher's lap who gasps when my girl's incredible body grinds against hers with one hip roll.

"Please. I want to come, make me come!" The desperation from Mrs.Sullivan reeks. I'm an idiot for ever hooking up with her.

"You're dying to come, aren't you?" Tillie asks, leaning forward to skim her lips along the other woman's mouth.

I've had enough, I'm about to make my presence known to stop this and bruise her fucking ass for kissing someone who isn't me or the guys.

"It's killing me. Touch me. Please, touch my pussy." Mrs.-Sullivan throws her head back, letting out a moan as Tillie drags her fingers down fake breasts and stomach, stopping just shy of our teacher's underwear.

"I'll kill you," Tillie whispers seriously, bringing her other hand that was hiding behind her back forward and wrapping the cord quickly around Mrs.Sullivan's neck before she knows what's happening.

"Wha–what are you doing?!" The pathetic teacher who preys on her students just asked the dumbest question known to mankind.

She should have realized the whole time she's been in the classroom alone with a very, very dangerous woman. Being a predator, having sex with her students, and getting away with it made her think she's invincible. Guess she's about to learn she's not.

"I wouldn't touch your dried-up cunt with a ten-foot pole, you fucking pedo. You think I'd just let it slide that you've touched what's mine and eye fuck him every chance you get?" Tillie grits out between her teeth, tightening the cord around Mrs.Sullivan's throat until her face starts turning an ugly shade of purple while she struggles.

A small chuckle slips past my lips, causing Tillie's head to whip around with murder in her glare before she realizes it's me.

"Little bitch, you surprise me at every turn. Don't ever change." I'm completely honest, I love this badass Goddess before me.

I stride across the room with my hands in my pockets and whistle when I glance over her shoulder at the panicked, wide eyes of Mrs.Sullivan who looks at me like I'm going to save her.

"This isn't how it looks." Tillie bats innocent, brown eyes up at me, her fist pulling the cord tighter while the pedo claws at her throat as her air supply is suddenly blocked.

"You don't say? Looks to me like you're trying to kill your teacher." I rub my hand across my mouth, hiding my smile.

"Thank God. I thought you would think I was cheating on you guys." Her shoulders relax and she smiles shyly up at me with a blush coloring her tan cheeks.

"I'm sorry but you can't kill her. Dead teacher brings the news station to the school and Franco wouldn't be pleased about that." I huff out a breath, sad I'm ruining her fun but maybe I can help have fun another way without killing anyone.

"Fuckin Franco." She growls under her breath and starts to let go of the cord with a sigh until I place my hand over hers to stop her.

"I have an idea," I say, eyeing the flag pole behind the desk.

"And just like that, I'm suddenly scared," Tillie jokes, easing off Mrs.Sullivan's lap but keeping her in place by not loosening the cord. "Well?"

I wink at her and kick the chair Mrs.Sullivan is sitting in back, the wheels rolling her into the wall right under the flag-pole. The cord loosens for a second as it slips from Tillie's grip and the only sound you can hear is gasping breaths as someone's air supply returns and a sob escapes her pedo lips. I don't waste time. I walk behind her chair and grab the loose piece of the cord, pulling it until Mrs.Sullivan is wiggling like a soon to be dead fish. I keep pulling until I can reach high up to wrap the cord around the pole. If she holds still, she won't choke too much but if she keeps kicking and wiggling, I'd give her about five minutes before she kills herself.

"I wouldn't move if I were you. It doesn't take long for all the oxygen to leave the brain as you choke to death." My words must have gotten through to her because she stops struggling but keeps sobbing, her chest heaving for breath.

"Now what?" Tillie asks from behind me and when I turn around, she's up on the desk again, swinging her legs back and forth.

I reach out for her, placing both of the palms of my hands on her cheeks, and gaze at her upturned face.

"Now, I confess my undying love to this amazing, beautiful, badass, little bitch." I speak from the heart, telling the truth as I look into her shining, brown eyes.

"Make me yours." She grabs my vest and pulls me into a kiss that almost has my knees buckling.

I trace the indent of her lips, sliding my tongue along the

crease of her bottom lip. A deep groan slips out of my mouth at the taste of her strawberry chapstick, fresh peppermint from her toothpaste, and the just Tillie taste that's natural, sweet. It's addicting. She opens her mouth on a moan, pulling me closer until she can wrap her legs around my waist. I slide my tongue against hers, lips locked together and only coming up for air until my nose is skimming the other side of hers. Her skirt gathers around her hips as she leans back with a deep exhale, and quickly works my belt and jeans undone as if she's as desperate as I am to feel her.

We both ignore the loud sobbing behind me and I couldn't care less if the fucking teacher can see us fucking. She'll see me claiming my girl.

Tillie yanks my jeans down to my thighs and scoots to the edge of the desk, pulling her panties to the side so I can see how glistening wet her pussy is. Dripping and all mine to fuck. This time, she doesn't look at my cock as if it's going to attack her, she looks hungry as hell as she stares at my hard length.

"You have the biggest dick, I swear. Put your cock in me right now," she bosses me, gripping the base of my cock to guide it towards her pussy, rubbing the pulsing tip along her clit and pleasuring herself that has me hanging by a thread.

"You really are a bitch," I growl out, knocking her hand away, and line up at her sopping wet, beautiful pussy, watching as my dick slowly sinks into her.

"Only your bitch," she pants out, her mouth hanging open in the perfect O as she watches my cock slide halfway in and slides out again, glistening with her juices. I keep working her until I sink all the way in, sending a prayer to the man above that he sent me a woman to fit all nine inches of me.

"You feel so good." I groan, pulling out slowly halfway

before slamming back inside her with a quick snap of my hips.

"Less talking, more fucking, Daddy." She gasps as I growl, grabbing the back of her thighs to spread her wider and fucking her until the only sound coming out of her delicious mouth are moans.

She fucking knows what calling me her Daddy does to me.

The sound of our skin slapping together fills the classroom, blocking out the sobbing behind me. I fuck her hard and fast, glancing down to watch my cock slide in and out of her wet pussy. She grabs my biceps as I pick up the pace, hitting deep inside that has her back aching and the desk screeching across the room from the rough pounding I'm giving her. She suddenly sits up straight, clasping her legs around my waist and rolling her hips to meet me stroke for stroke. Wanting to feel her breasts against my chest, I pick her up under her ass and turn us around, walking towards the whiteboard. Her back slams against it, the whole thing rattling as I continue to fuck her. She wraps her hands around the back of my neck and starts to bounce as I grab her hips to make her go faster. My groan is loud even to my own ears. It feels so damn good.

"Just like that, little bitch. Squeeze my cock with your fucking tight pussy." I lean my forehead into her neck, releasing one hand from her ass to slide between our bodies until my thumb is circling her clit while the rest of my hand is squeezing her pussy.

"Dalton, I'm going to come! Fill me up with your cum!" she cries out, her eyes meeting mine as I lean back to watch her face twist into rapture.

It takes me a second to realize what she just said. I didn't expect to fuck her walking into the classroom or her finally giving me the go-ahead to cum. I would have pleasured my girl even if my balls turned bluer and embraced the pain of a hard cock until she says I can cum.

"You sure?" I grunt out, watching her face as her eyes widen, her lips falling open as her pussy clenches my cock in a tight as fuck grip.

"Yesss. Yes. Oh God. Yes, Daddy!" She scratches at my back with her nails digging in deep as her body trembles from head to toe violently and her eyes roll to the back of her head.

Watching her come, feeling her squirting all over my cock, it's the most beautiful thing I've ever seen and felt on my cock. I can't hold back anymore. My head arches back, exposing my neck as I groan just as the first burst of pent-up cum coats her insides, shot after shot. She leans forward, biting my Adam's apple and licking up my neck until she places moaning kisses on my lips when I glance back down at her. For the first time in my life, I think my knees are fucking weak after sex. She's killed me.

"Fuck. You're incredible," I pant out, trying to catch my breath as she nuzzles into my chest with a content sigh.

"I needed that. Needed you," she says, placing a kiss on my chest before pulling away and looking back up at me. "I love you, Dalton."

My heart was already racing but it picks up speed until it feels like I'm going to burst. Is that what love does? Makes it feel like you're dying but living for the first time in your life? Looking at her face, her brown eyes that have a small speck of green... I know it's real. She's it for me.

"I'd give up my bike for you, Tillie. That's how much I love you." I crack a smile when she smacks my chest, unwrapping her legs from mine as I let her down. "Seriously though, you're everything to me."

"I know," she says cheekily, giggling before stretching on

her tiptoes to place a kiss on my cheek as I pretend to scowl at her.

I fix my jeans, buckling my belt as she smooths her skirt down and slips her underwear off with a grimace. My cock hardens again seeing her panties soaked with my cum and hers. I can't fuck her again, the room is about to start filling up with students any minute. Maybe I can convince her into a janitor's closet? Her cum is still coating my cock and soaking into my skin from how hard she squirted. Even my boots and the floor where we were fucking is wet. My cock doesn't care that it was just in a warm home in her juicy pussy, it wants back in.

Fuck. Down, boy.

I argue with my dick, knowing he can wait. I see a lot of fucking in my future with my little bitch. Tillie glances at her underwear with an arched brow as she smoothes her skirt back into place and looks slowly over at Mrs.Sullivan with a wicked gleam in her eyes. I almost forgot about her in the corner. Her face is red, mascara darkened under her eyes like a raccoon from all the sobbing she's been doing. She's so dramatic. It's not like we killed her.

"Seems you live for another day. You don't get to have him." Tillie points over her shoulder at me as she goes to stand in front of Mrs.Sullivan. "You don't get anyone. I'm going to make sure the world knows you're a pedo cunt."

I watch in amusement, leaning against the whiteboard with my arms crossed as Tillie pries open Mrs.Sullivan's mouth in a strong grip and shoves her cream-filled panties into the pedo's mouth. I walk over and untie her from the pole, quickly securing her hands behind her back by tying them to the chair. Muffled words try to work around the gag as she watches Tillie turn towards her desk to open drawers until she hums in approval at whatever she was looking for. She blocks my view as she leans her face in front of Mrs.Sullivan's with something in her hand. A few seconds go by before she leans away and nods her head in approval. The bell rings just as I see what she did.

Pedo is written across Mrs.Sullivan's forehead and on her chest in sharpie says *I like them young.*

At the time, I never really thought about it. I just wanted to sink my dick into an available pussy to just forget about everything in life. I may have flirted with my teacher but she could have put a stop to it at any time. She didn't.

"Feel better?" I ask Tillie, placing my arm over her shoulders and pushing students out of our way with my other hand as they start to fill up the classroom.

The first scream pierces my ears just as we pass through the door followed by gasps of shocked students. I don't bother glancing back, I see a teacher running in our direction to see what's happening. I bet students are already filming and everyone will know before the day is over what kind of person Mrs.Sullivan is.

"I feel really fucking good. And Hungry." Tillie smirks, looking happy.

That's my little bitch. Kicking ass and fucking me weak.

What a woman.

# CHAPTER 14

Dom

It's almost too easy. Does Franco think hiring a few guards with big guns at his gates will protect him from the outside world?

"All clear on the left perimeter," one of Franco's men mutters into a radio, passing right by without seeing me, just a few feet away from him.

That pisses me off to no end. My queen is behind these gates being protected by a bunch of fucking idiots. The urge to steal her away, even if she's fighting me, always comes on strong when I see shit like this.

Dressed in all black from the neck down, I sneak out of the shadows by the fence that's surrounded by shrubbery and silently walk behind him until I'm practically breathing down his neck.

"El tonto." Calling the guard a fool is probably the nicest thing I've ever said in Spanish.

Before he can turn around, I wrap my forearm around his neck and squeeze. Choking the life out of him makes me feel better, one less idiot in the world and it's a big fuck you to Franco when they find his body tomorrow morning. He breathes his last breath, his body going slack in my grip and I quietly drag him over to the bushes. Kicking his feet into the greenery, I straighten and crack my neck side to side while brushing dirt off my expensive Adolfo Dominguez suit. Just because I came from the hood doesn't mean I can't dress in style. I'm setting an example for my gang and enemies.

Don't fucking mess with me, I'll put a bullet in your head while wearing a suit that cost a couple grand. It's good for my men to see a strong leader that will set the path for the next generation.

I button my black jacket, smooth out the wrinkles and walk across the yard towards the front door calmly like I own Franco's house. One day I just might. I'll take everything away from him. My eyes narrow on the door handle as it turns easily under my hands. I'm going to have to bash Logan's head in too. If anything happens to Tillie under his roof because of their stupidity, I'll burn his house down with him inside. Striding to the staircase on silent feet, I grab the banister and take the stairs two at a time.

My lips twitch when I hear laughter coming from Tillie's bedroom. I could find her room with my eyes closed, it's that easy for me. Scoping out Franco's house for years, standing over his bed as he slept peacefully, wondering if that was going to be the moment I killed him...It became an obsession of mine to fuck with Franco without him knowing I could effortlessly get to him anytime I want to. I don't want him to have an easy way out, I want his world to crash and burn around him as he begs for mercy at my feet.

"This one video has thousands of views already. Mrs.Sullivan was fired and dragged out of school in handcuffs by two officers." Tey snickers in delight, I want to punch his face in when I see him and Tillie's heads together on her bed as they stare at his phone.

The fucker sent me a text today with only two words and the video he's probably watching now. *Tillie's work.* I was in the middle of selling a new product of Mary Jane that gets you high within minutes to some new investors but the moment I clicked play on the video, I was canceling my meeting with no explanation. The investors flew all the way from New York. The Marijuana I distribute is grown all over Mexico and on some farms in California. It's the best shit you can get on the market. I didn't care about any of that though when I opened my phone. I drove two hours, going faster than the speed limit and cursing myself for being on the farm so far away from the city. Which leads me back to now, sneaking into Russo's home to make sure my queen is okay.

I need a fucking smoke.

"Jesus H. Christ! How the hell did you get in?" Logan shouts, cursing up a blue streak of Italian and standing up from a chaise lounge by the window the moment he sees me leaning in the open doorway.

It's too bad we don't see eye to eye and he's been brain-washed by his father, otherwise, I might actually like him. Aggressive, angry Italian, dressed in expensive Italian clothes, and he's not a bad shot with his Glock.

"Maybe you should lock your front door and no one would sneak into your house without your knowledge," I reply back smoothly, pulling out a small metal case from my back pocket.

"He killed one of your father's henchmen. Almost missed him on the feed," Nicky speaks up, his almond-shaped eyes glancing up from the computer on his lap and locking with mine.

Dare I say he looks impressed?

I like this one even if his sperm donor is Jin.

"Remind me to upgrade my security system," Dalton grumbles, laying back at the end of Tillie's bed with his arm over his head.

"You have a death wish don't you?" Logan paces back and forth. If he doesn't quit, he might leave a hole in the rug.

"Are you going to kill me, Russo, or is daddy dearest?" I ask in a harsh voice, flicking my lighter and inhaling deeply as I put the joint to my lips.

"If you pass that around, I'll tie up Logan if he tries to kill you." Tey sizes Logan up, smirking as his amigo glares at him before turning his gaze towards me.

They say you can see into the soul of someone by just looking in their eyes but when you look in this crazy fucker's eyes, you don't see a damn thing. His bright, blue gaze is eerie and I can't even keep eye contact without getting a shiver down my back.

"Why not? It's my new product, enjoy." I take one more puff and walk over to the bed, my gaze locking with Tillie's as she smiles up at me.

Tey takes the joint out of my hand, inhaling in bliss as I lean over him and gently grab Tillie's jaw. She opens her mouth under the pressure of my fingers and I exhale smoke from my mouth and into hers, my lips pressed lightly against her exquisite, parted lips.

She coughs a little as I pull away, blinking rapidly as she holds her breath and blows out the rest of the smoke from her mouth before relaxing back into Tey's chest with a content sigh.

"That's some good shit, my brother. I think I'll keep you." Tey grins dreamily, pulling Tillie closer into his chest.

"Fuck it, it's been a long day. Give me some." Logan snatches the joint out of Tey's hand and continues pacing while exhaling towards the ceiling.

"How was your day, mama?" I ask casually, grabbing her desk chair and flipping it around to straddle it.

"Oh, you know. Same old, same old. Just violence and fucking, a normal day." She waves her hand and looks towards the end of the bed at Dalton with a smirk.

"I like normal days." Dalton chuckles around a yawn and winks at her before shutting his eyes again.

"She kissed her teacher, Mrs.Sullivan, fucked Dalton in front of her, and got said teacher arrested all in one day," Nicky says in a bored tone, not bothering to look up as he types on his laptop like a maniac.

I heard he's good with a computer but I have yet to see that skill set of his. That's a bit worrisome for me, what if he hacked into my shit? I narrow my eyes at him, seeing it's pointless as he doesn't glance up. His fingers stall for a split-second on the keyboard as Tey starts running his fingers through Nicky's hair. Watching them for a while now, seeing the sexual tension even from afar, it's about time they started acting on it. Love is love and I'm all for it. My gaze trails back to Tillie only to find her gaze locked on mine with a tilt of her head.

"No comment?" she asks.

"No. I expect nothing less from my queen." My eyes become hooded, picturing her fucking up people's lives while enjoying herself.

"Just like that?" She continues to stare at me like I'm a mystery.

"Just like that." I shrug, crossing my arms over the top of her desk chair.

"No more kissing anyone else outside of your harem, little bitch," Dalton mutters sleepily.

No wonder he's denying a joint, he looks seconds from passing out. He fucked our girl to next Sunday and the fact that he is also now Prez... Life fucks you in the ass some days, but on good days there's pussy like Tillie's to sink yourself inside to escape everything else.

Her face grimaces as she shudders, likely from remembering kissing her teacher before she watches Logan pace the room through hooded, high eyes.

"Do it again and I'll cuff you to the bed," Nicky threatens with a grin like he enjoys that idea and finally glances up from his laptop. "Since we are all here and Franco has taken Diana to a charity dinner, now is the perfect time to discuss some things I've found."

Logan stops pacing, standing at the end of the bed with his arms crossed. This will be interesting, I wonder if they took my advice to not trust Franco and start digging deeper.

"Just get it over with and tell me who I have to kill," Tey says, nuzzling Tillie's hair with his eyes closed.

I bet he could kill someone with his eyes closed and go for ice cream right after. I shift my gaze back to Nicky and see him staring at me with a knowing glint in his eyes.

"Dom was right. You did give some bread crumbs to follow at the rave." Nicky shuts his laptop, takes a deep breath, and grabs Tillie's hand in his like he needs the extra strength. She is the strongest woman I know, I don't blame him for seeking her comfort. "Franco is now in the skin business. Has been for months," Nicky says without emotion but squeezes Tillie's hand harder.

"I can't say I'm surprised. It was only a matter of time. What else did you learn from the hard drive I gave you?" Logan's facial expression hardens, preparing himself for whatever else the hacker is going to say.

"As you already know, Jin has requested that Tillie dance at the auction. I've seen the guest list and the Los Muerte leader, Carlos, is going." After Nicky delivers that bit of news that I already know, I lean forward to rest my chin on my forearms to watch the show.

"That son of a bitch! What is he doing?! I'm going to kill him! Fucking kill him!" Logan pulls at his neatly styled hair that always seems to never be out of place and spins around, punching the wall.

Tillie untangles herself between Tey and Nicky, climbing

over Dalton at the end of the bed to stand behind Logan as he stares at the hole in the wall. She places her hand on his heaving back and when he doesn't react, she plasters her body against his from behind while wrapping her arms around him. My eyebrows reach my hairline as I see him take a deep breath, gaining control of himself by just her touch alone. He turns around and wraps his arms around her like he's never letting go. I huff out a breath when a surge of jealousy goes through me but it quickly calms when I see the way she stares up at him. The way she stares at all of us. She cares about these guys, us, even though at times I want to steal her away, she's good for them. For all of us.

"It's going to be okay. We'll figure it out together. I need you to listen to this part." She taps his temple with her index finger and places her hand over his heart. "And not this place. We have to think smart about this. What does Franco gain from this?"

"Power. All the power. Do you get it yet? Your shipments aren't missing, it's being stolen from right under your noses by Franco this whole time. Timing is key to everything and if he ordered you to take out the leader of Los Muerte by accusing them of stealing, what would you do?" I ask Logan, seeing the puzzle pieces start clicking together.

"I'd do it without questions. A rivalry breaks out, gang against gang. No one is left standing except Franco." Logan looks flabbergasted like he was just knocked off his feet, squeezing Tillie one more time before letting go to pace again.

"He's dipping his hands into all aspects. Gangs and motorcycle clubs. I wonder if my dad suspected anything? Does Jin? What is your father doing with all the guns he stole from my club?!" Dalton suddenly sits up, practically shouting and looking very awake.

"I would think, probably selling them to each gang for a

full-on war in the streets." I stroke my jaw, seeing that happening and many lives being lost, civilians too.

"Holy shit." Tey grabs his legendary knife out of his boot and swirls it between his fingers as he stares off into space.

"Nothing gets past my father. Nothing," Nicky says, banging the back of his head against the headboard as he stares up at the ceiling.

"You know Jin used to have my father sell on the streets for him right?" Everyone turns towards me as I casually drop that bit of information, something that's always bugged me.

"What are you saying?" Nicky asks darkly, sitting up as his full attention focuses on me.

"You're right. Jin has always had eyes and ears everywhere. You never thought it was suspicious that the man he did cocaine and heroin business with suddenly gets accused of murdering a cop's wife who was looking into the coming and goings of drugs made by Jin's men?" All the blood drains from Nicky's face, his gaze darting over to Logan who hasn't said a word.

"Those drugs were never linked back to Jin. It was coming from your father's meth houses. Franco did his research, undercover for months before my mother was murdered by your father." Logan strides over to me with his fists clenched, but gets interrupted by an angry, little Latino.

"Hold on a second. Why do you think Jin supplied drugs to your father's gang?" Tillie turns to me, blocking Logan's path with her hands on her hips.

"Because I used to see Jin come visit the house I grew up in," I reply, thinking back to my hiding spot on the staircase whenever my father had *guests* come over.

"I want this product on the streets and sold within two days. All of it." A man in an expensive suit stands in the middle of our living room with his back turned towards me.

Even I knew he was loaded, probably had so much money he

didn't know what to do with it. His shoes shone, pressed suit without a wrinkle, and slicked back hair. This man didn't belong in our rundown house. At twelve years old, I could feel the tension coming off him that told me he was dangerous. His wide shoulders were relaxed while he stared down my father as if he didn't fear anything because he was the thing to fear.

"That's not enough time. I can't—" My dad rubbed at his mustache, a sign he did when he was nervous.

It wasn't often my dad became nervous, he usually instilled fear into people. But with this guy, he was sweating and glancing around so he didn't have to look into the man's eyes.

"You can or I will find someone else to run my drugs." The stranger said, his voice deep and threatening that had me leaning farther into the staircase so he couldn't see me.

"Of course. I won't disappoint you, Jin." My dad cleared his throat, taking a step back as Jin stepped towards him.

"See that you don't," Jin said, waiting a few seconds in silence before turning towards the front door.

His almond-shaped, brown eyes flicked up at my hiding spot as if he knew I was there the whole time. He stared at me with a grin as he walked by, his face smooth and young looking compared to my dad. Though he had a streak of grey hair near his temple, telling me he wasn't young by any means. Appearances are deceiving, I knew that. A snake could hold still, staring you right in the eye, trying to distract you by the beautiful scales that glistened in the sun and never giving you a warning it was going to attack you until it was too late. That's what this Jin man reminded me of.

A snake.

"If you're saying what I think you are..." Nicky speaks up, never taking his gaze off Logan, who stares right back at him.

"We've been lied to. Everything I was taught to hate, to destroy was all for nothing. Absolutely nothing," Logan whispers, walking away to go stare out the window with his back turned towards us.

"Can someone tell me what's going on?" Tillie glances around at all of us, looking for answers that's about to shatter their reality.

"Jin came for Franco when he was at his weakest, planting a seed in his mind," I reply, clearing my throat when it becomes too thick to speak.

"I wonder if Franco knows." Dalton sits there in stunned silence, his gaze staring off into space.

"Knows what?!" Frustration is clear in Tillie's voice as we try to skirt around from actually saying it out loud.

"If it's true, that means when Franco was undercover looking into the drugs that came from Jin all along... Dom's father could have been set up. The possibility that it's been Jin this whole time," Dalton explains aloud, shaking his head as if he can't wrap his mind around it.

It took me a lot of time to come to that conclusion too. Many years, a whisper in the back of my head telling me nothing was adding up. It wasn't until the money started flowing, inviting myself to social events to watch the people that put on an act and are completely different behind closed doors that my path led me straight to Jin after so many years. It's like the puzzle pieces came all together, clicking into place as memories flooded my senses.

"My dad wasn't a good man by any means but he wouldn't have killed a woman who had a child waiting for her at home. Family meant something to him," I mutter out loud, almost startled when Tillie palms my cheek as I got lost in my thoughts.

"What does this mean?" Tillie questions, seeing right through all the hurt and anger that's been locked inside me for so many years.

"Jin," Nicky says flatly, getting up from the bed to stand behind Logan. "It's possible that he could be the one responsible for your mother's death. A set up from the beginning."

Tillie gasps, her eyes going wide as she finally sees it. Her red eyes flood with tears as she leans down to kiss my forehead. My eyes drift closed, absorbing the way she's healing me inside and out. It's like she's taking all my pain whether I want her to or not. Finally, after so many years, the truth is coming to the surface and I won't be fighting my battles alone anymore.

My Queen.

She pulls back with a sad smile and crosses the room to Logan, stopping at his side while glancing out the window without saying a word. She only reaches for his hand, offering her support.

"You're not going to that auction, both of you. I'll slaughter anyone from limb to limb who stands in my way," Tey says seriously. I think it's the first time I've seen him without a grin on his face.

"What choice do we have?" Nicky continues to stare at the back of Logan's head with stiff shoulders.

I can understand where he's coming from. A weight bigger than he can handle now rests on Nicky's shoulders. One of his best friends finds out his father is responsible for killing Helen... The guilt starts eating you alive even though you didn't pull the trigger.

"We can't run. We all have too many responsibilities and people counting on us," Dalton growls out, resting his head in his hands.

He's right. Each of us has someone counting on us. The families that stand before our ruling, putting food on their tables and a roof over their heads.

"No." Logan lifts Tillie's hand and kisses her knuckles before letting go and turning around to face us. "No running. It ends right where it began. Everyone who's wronged us, hurt our girl, ripped families apart... they answer to us." He steps forward, laying his hand on Nicky's shoulder as he stares into his eyes.

"They will pay," Nicky speaks up in a dark, deep voice, nodding once before walking back to his laptop with purpose and a murderous glint in his eyes.

"In blood." A sinister grin starts spreading across Tey's mouth. I wouldn't be surprised if the crazy fucker bathed in his enemy's blood with a rubber ducky in the mornings.

"Where do we begin? The club will stand behind me on this. They want blood spilled ever since Pike was murdered. Payne's death wasn't enough for killing their Prez," Dalton says with a grunt, cracking his big fists and straightening his leather vest while smoothing out his facial expression until it's almost blank.

I would not want to be the man who sees those fists heading towards my face. I can hold my own but Dalton has hammer fists that could probably kill a man. I'm betting that since Pike died, he's been gunning for Demon Jokers' blood. Both for his father's death and for Tillie's suffering. I'm right beside him on the last part. I shake my head to clear it, turning my gaze to Tillie, watching as she takes this all in without an emotion on her pretty face.

"Mama, you haven't said anything. What's going on in that head of yours?" I question, noticing the guys going silent as we all stare at her.

"I'm just beginning to realize how connected we all are. I thought I wanted to run from this life but instead of running away, I'm running towards the violence." Her voice comes out soft but strong, I'm thinking we've only just glimpsed, on the outside, how incredibly strong our girl is.

"Does that thought scare you?" Logan glances down at her, his brow raised, challenging her which she just meets head-on, and crosses her arms while glaring up at him.

"No. It gives me life." She starts to grin, finally showing her true colors.

"Hey, fucker, where do you stand?" Tey asks me before quickly glancing at my queen and grinning like a loon as he blows Tillie a kiss then directs his crazy eyes back on me.

I meet his blue gaze in a stare down without blinking, my dark eyes clashing with his. One of us may appear angelic while the other is sinister but inside we both bleed red. Guess that makes me crazy too.

"It could be the weed talking, it seems to make you all sappy but fuck it. I'm in. We'll take them all down together even if I have to put up with your annoying, dramatic ass." I give Logan a head nod, chuckling as his upper lip curls in disgust.

Dramatic but at least we are on the same page.

I can work just fine alongside him, kill everyone who stands in our path and make sure my queen is protected. I only have one small problem with him right now and that's him thinking he can hurt Tillie. He doesn't know it yet but his little adventures to my clubs weren't just watched by me. Seems a reporter loves to follow him around and he's going to pay dearly when Tillie finds out what he did. I'll be right here for my queen, not hesitating if she wants him dead. He better fix his wrong before she finds out herself.

CHAPTER 15

Tillie

Why does it feel like I'm death walking? Whose idea was it to smoke weed during a weekday and stay up half the night trying to come up with a plan that might involve one of us, or all of us, getting killed?

I went to bed anxious, worried about what consequences our actions might cause but I'm done sitting back. I sat back and watched someone control my future without ever saying anything because it was pointless when I never had a say. I can see it so clearly now, no one will decide how I live my life but me. The guys weren't kidding about having a sleepover, even Dom stayed, only leaving before the sun rose. Something about him stalking in the shadows, coming and going as he pleases is a big turn-on for me. I'm really glad Uncle Ri– I mean Rig taught me Spanish. The way Dom rolls his R's... The beautiful, graceful language slipping out of his mouth like honey had me blushing like a virgin. It pissed Logan off to no end seeing the way the smooth talker affected me. It had him shouting in loud Italian while gesturing his hands angrily. It's unfortunate I don't understand what he's saying but it doesn't take a genius to figure out what curse words he was shouting at Dom. Still hot though.

I laughed until my stomach hurt, watching them go back

and forth with insults. I think it was a way to ease the tension we all seemed to be under. That's what family does, sticks together through thick and thin. I couldn't be happier even if sadness and rage lay heavily in my gut. I'm letting fate take the wheel for once, knowing deep down it's going to lead us down a path of murder and mayhem. That thought doesn't scare me, I think I've been spending too much time with Tey because I'm actually looking forward to killing all the sick fucks out there. I really do belong to these guys, fitting right in like a puzzle piece, and I wouldn't change it for anything. This is bliss. I woke up this morning, overly hot but didn't care. I soaked in the bliss of being surrounded by my guys. Tey had his arm thrown over my waist, snuggled into my side as Nicky hugged him from behind like the big spoon. Dalton lay on my other side, his big biceps acting as my pillow. His face was relaxed, long lashes framing his cheeks. I was almost afraid to move in case he woke up. He's been working hard, putting aside his grief for Pike but that will catch up to him eventually and when it does hopefully he's ready to come to terms that his old man really is gone. I'll be right here to get him through it. Yesterday was his last day of school, he made the right decision even though I'll miss seeing him there. I can understand running a motorcycle club comes first because that's family and everyone is counting on him.

I stayed still for a long time, looking at each of my guys as they slept. I couldn't see Logan's face but he kept sighing in contentment in his sleep. He slept between my legs, resting his head on the bare skin of my stomach. I kept running my fingers through his hair as the sun rose, lighting up my bedroom just in time for me to see Dom rise from the chaise lounge. He wouldn't sleep, kept shaking his head as I tried to get him to come to bed. He said he wanted to watch over me, making sure I knew that no one was getting to me with him guarding our backs as sleep overtook me.

I've been walking around school all day like a zombie but I've never felt lighter inside. A weight was lifted that's been settled on my shoulders for as long as I can remember. I slept without a nightmare, dreaming of big cocks because I'm apparently sex crazy now. I've never felt so comfortable closing my eyes at night and getting a full amount of sleep. It's probably from being surrounded by men that will take a bullet for me. I didn't wake up or move around, not even once. Nothing was going to take away this feeling from me. I won't let the cramps in my lower stomach stop my good mood. Although starting my period in the middle of class isn't ideal, I'm taking care of it right now sitting in the girl's bathroom stall.

Fucking period.

Why does my period have to make an appearance out of the blue without a warning? Another pair of underwear ruined as I clean myself up and curse when I see there isn't a tampon in my backpack. I'll just ask if another girl comes in if I can have one. For now, I'll hide in the stall until my embarrassment fades. I couldn't hide that aunt Flo came to visit me. At least my skirt is black but my white silk underwear can't hide the fact.

Do you know how difficult it is to check if the feeling of wetness between your legs is mother nature cursing you or accidentally peeing your pants? It's not easy. Tey was sitting next to me in class and kept giving me confused looks as I kept wiggling in my seat and dropping a pencil under my desk to look up my skirt. A spot of bright blood stained the front of my panties. I fucking hate aunt flo with a passion, she can go suck it. I folded my hands around my waist as I sat up, taking a deep breath as pain shot through my abdomen. I quickly picked up my backpack off the floor and slipped out of my seat sideways just in case my period seeped through the back of my skirt. The confusion cleared from Tey's face, as a shit eating grin spread across his lips, finally realizing what was wrong as my cheeks turned red. I took a bathroom pass and almost ran out of the class, feeling the heat of Tey's gaze on my retreating back.

How embarrassing. I don't even know why I'm embarrassed, it's a fucking natural thing but still. Maybe it's the carnal desire that overtook Tey's face? I know he loves blood, fascinated by it but he wasn't serious about before... right? Wanting to have dirty, bloody sex with me? The thought excites me to the point of demanding him to fuck me right now and makes me wary too. What if he gets disgusted?

Ugh. Am I really thinking of having sex with Tey while hiding in the girls' bathroom? At least it's the smallest worry in my life, it could be worse.

The girls' bathroom door opens, bringing in the sound of laughter of girls and the clicks of heels. I'm about to open the door to see if anyone can spare a tampon but *her* voice stops me.

"Can you believe she walks around here like she owns the place, hanging off Logan like a whore?" Paris says in a disgusted tone.

I peek through the stall crack, seeing her applying lipgloss in the mirror as her two sidekicks stand on either side of her doing the same thing. I roll my eyes, not having the patience for her today. I'm hungry, horny, and angry, so I don't want to deal with her bullshit today. She's been staying clear of me, but doesn't stop the dirty looks and smiles like she knows something I don't when we pass in the halls.

"I heard she's fucking all of them. Half the football team too," her friend says with a snicker, fluffing her hair in the mirror.

"It's really pathetic actually. She's hanging off my boyfriend's arm when everyone knows he's dating me.

Logan's just playing her, he told me so." Paris flips her hair over her shoulder before blowing a kiss at her reflection.

My stomach drops, fists clenching at my sides and I've heard just about enough out of her lying mouth. I fling the door open, startling them as they shriek until they see me standing in the open stall with my arms crossed over my chest.

"Stalk much?" Paris's other friend sneers. I can't seem to care to get to know their names.

"You know what is pathetic, Paris? You and how you continue to chase Logan when he obviously doesn't want you. Keep spreading rumors, I don't give a fuck because I'm the one warming Logan's bed at night. Actually, all of them. So yeah, I'm a slut. Their slut." I grin as her face contorts into rage, her cheeks turning red as her friends go silent.

"My God. You're so blind and easy to spread your legs to any guy it would seem. You are nothing but trash. Logan realizes that and he'll drop you once he's done with you. I'll be here, waiting for him to return to me like he always does." Paris steps close, pulling out her cellphone, and shoves it in my face while looking smug as hell.

I pull my gaze away from her and blink a couple of times as the image in front of me on the screen starts to make sense. I can distantly hear the girls giggling but my whole focus narrows on the image of Paris and the two guys surrounding her on a red velvet couch that looks familiar. Dom's club. My eyes scan the article by Elle Walker, a journalist.

What is this? It can't be real. Logan promised me... but you can't deny what's right in front of your face.

Both Logan and Nicky are on either side of her, crowded close like lovers. Paris has her hand on Logan's leg as it looks like he's whispering something in her ear with a smile on her face. Nicky's chest is pressed up against her back, his hand wrapped around the back of her neck as he stares at the couple in front of him with a small grin stretched across his thick lips.

Nicky hardly ever smiles. God. Can this really be happening? Does Tey know about this? I feel like a fool, staring at the article that just goes on and on about Franco's son not setting a good example since his father might be putting his hat into the next election. I don't care about any of that.

"See? You are just a game to pass the time," Paris sneers in my face, smirking when she sees my eyes water until I blink the tears away. "I was surprised Nicky has taken an interest in me since he has a thing for dicks. Disgusting."

Her friends laugh, making crude jokes and making fun of Nicky. I feel my pulse pounding, a whooshing in my ear as if I have my head dunked under water.

"What the fuck did you just say?" My body is locked tight as a bowstring, all my focus zeroing on Paris.

"You heard me, skank." Her voice is arrogant, making me feel pissed off and repulsed by her behavior.

She snatches her phone out of my frozen fingers as she turns back to the mirror, playing with her hair and laughing with her friends as I stand behind her. I can handle her shoving her relationship with Logan in my face, I'll cry about it later under my covers but to make fun of someone for loving another person... It's wrong. The whole thing makes me mad, furious that I make my decision to kick her snooty, hypocrite ass. I don't think, I just react.

Her scream echoes around the bathroom as I grab her by the back of her head, my fist tight in her hair. There's just something therapeutic about slamming her plastic surgery nose in the mirror, her face is squished and smeared with blood from the cut at her temple.

"I've had enough of your jealousy and nasty attitude. Should I just kill you now?" I lean down and whisper in her ear, watching her eyes widen as she struggles in my grip.

Her two friends intervene, pulling me off Paris who turns around with her lip curled as she dives at me. The two girls scream as we go down in a tangle of limbs the moment Paris attacks me with her body, scratching her nails down my face hard enough to draw blood. I don't care at the moment, I want this bitch to pay for everything she's done since I first met her. Her two friends get up and scramble to the door, leaving me and Paris rolling on the floor as I pull my fists back to punch her in the face. Her elbow catches my lip, splitting it open as I manage to roll on top of her and swing my fists until she stops fighting back.

Arms wrap around me from behind, pulling me off a passed out Paris and I kick my legs, yelling as I try to get out of their hold.

"Calm down, killer. It's just me," Tey grunts out in my ear while tightening his arms around my waist. I try to kick his shin from behind, but he doesn't let up.

My body goes slack in his grip the moment it clicks with me that he's holding me back from committing murder in the girls' school bathroom. I pant for breath, staring down at Paris, and manage to kick her in the gut one more time before Tey pulls us away with a dark chuckle.

"Not that I don't disapprove but what did she do to make you beat her unconscious?" Tey gently sets me down on the bathroom counter, caging me between his arms as he examines my face.

"You don't know what Logan and Nicky did last week with Paris?" Tey's eyes flicker towards mine with a confused look before he presses his thumb against my split lip.

"You can't believe everything that comes out of Paris's mouth when she's jealous of you." He clicks his tongue, shaking his head while looking over my messy hair and bloody face with a soft smile spreading over his plump lips.

"Tey... There are pictures on the internet by some journalist catching them at Dom's club with her. They looked pretty cozy," I mumble, hating how defended and hurt I sound.

Tey freezes, staring deep into my eyes and biting his lip ring as doubt crosses his facial expression. I gasp as he swings me up in his arms suddenly, throwing me over his shoulder like a caveman until my only view is his tight, muscular ass. He walks out of the bathroom, and down the hallways of the school without saying anything. The sun is bright and hot on my back as he strides outside and across the parking lot before stopping. He bends down and sets me on my feet, the blood rushing back to my head with a small wave of dizziness. I glance around and see him holding open the backseat door of Nicky's car, waiting for me to move.

"Get in." He gestures with a wave of his hand to the backseat.

I huff out a breath and climb in, scooting over when Tey follows after me while slamming the car door behind him. The silence is thick as we shut ourselves in the car, the blacked out windows adding to our privacy. I watch him rummage around in the middle console, pulling out wipes and turning back towards me. It's hard to read his expression, his eyes flicking between mine and back towards the smeared blood on my face that he slowly wipes away.

"You have no reason to believe me but, Tillie... We are all crazy for you. Whatever Logan and Nicky did, hear them out first before making up your mind. Promise me that please?" Tey leans back, cupping my cheek as he swipes his thumb back and forth over the corner of my split lip.

I don't know if I can do that. I've been burned so many times in life that there isn't much left inside me to feel any emotions. I think of my life without the guys in it and come up blank. Maybe the image the journalist caught isn't what it looks like? Can I really trust a word anyone says, especially

Logan? What more do I have to lose? At least I'll be able to get a real answer and know if this is where I'm meant to be.

"I'm scared. What if it's something I'm not ready to hear?" I stare at him, hoping he has an answer but he just shakes his head with a sigh.

"I don't know, kitten, but I know those guys. They would kill for you, die for you and that says something. Although I'm kind of pissed about them keeping secrets. Do you want to have some fun with me while getting revenge?" Tey starts to smile wickedly, leaning back in the seat with his legs spread and patting his lap.

I grimace and glance down at my thighs, suddenly feeling shy.

"I don't think that's a good idea." I turn my gaze out the window, wondering if I should make a break for it so I don't have to have this conversation.

"Why's that?" I hear the smile in his voice and bite my bottom lip.

"I'm, um, on my period," I quickly say, wanting to die right here and now.

It's so stupid. I shouldn't feel embarrassed by something so normal but I don't want to see his face turn into one of disgust.

"Get over here so I can make you feel good and I'll get angel wings at the same time. A win and win. I've been wanting to fuck you bloody. I thought our first time would be with Nicky but he deserves to be punished for keeping secrets. Next time though." Tey smirks at my wide eyes and open mouth.

He did not just say that!

He strikes before I can stop him, both of his hands slide around my waist and lift me up until I'm straddling his lap. My skirt gathers around my upper thighs, revealing my white, silk panties and the obvious red spot staining the front. I'm about to pull my skirt down to cover myself but he quickly grabs my wrists, pinning them to my sides.

"Trust me. You've been starring in my dreams at night just like this." His long eyelashes cast shadows over his sharp cheekbones as he glances down and releases my wrists to run the pad of his index finger over the blood.

A shiver runs down my spine at the feeling. I tilt my head back in pleasure as he grazes my clit again with the smallest brush of his finger. My hips shift in his lap, sliding back and forth over the thick cock that strains down his thigh and keeps rubbing me in the perfect spot each time I move my pussy over him. Our heavy breathing fills the car, my moans echoing back to me each time his finger glides over my sensitive clit.

"I want you, Tey," I moan, glancing at him to see him already staring at me.

He looks at me like I'm a Goddess, making me feel beautiful and special.

"I have something for you." He grins, shifting around as he reaches between our bodies to pull something out of his pocket.

I stop moving, crooking my head to the side in confusion as he unfolds a choker in his hand. My name is engraved into the leather, big and bold.

"What is this?" I ask warily, shifting my gaze back to his and wondering if he wants me to wear the choker like a dog so everyone sees the leash attached and the owner on the other end.

"I had it made at the mall. It's not what you think." He chuckles and kisses my lips real quick before pulling back. "It's for me. So anyone who looks at me knows who exactly has my body and soul. Nicky's name is on the back, I thought it was fitting so he can see it anytime he wants." He places the leather in my hand, waiting to see what I'll do with it as he relaxes back against the seat.

I bite my lip, seeing what this gift means. This is Tey showing his love, in a fucked-up way but it means everything to me. My hand trembles as I lift the choker and slide it behind his neck, clipping the clasp until my name is front and center for the world to see.

"I love you too. Would it make you happy if I had one with your name for my neck?" I trail my fingers down my neck with a smile, instantly frowning as he slowly shakes his head.

"No. Your name is already engraved on my heart." He grabs my hand and places it over the steady beat of his heart.

"Fuck." I blink rapidly, willing tears to not fall as all these men destroy me in the best way.

My fist clenches on his shirt and I pull him forward to smash my lips against his, the cold metal of his lip ring biting into my bottom lip. Blood begins to drip down my chin from reopening my split lip but I don't care. I can't get enough of him. Our tongues stroke against each in hunger, running along the stream of my mouth that makes me shiver from his pierced tongue. Over and over he meets me, not even coming up for air between kisses.

"Clothes off." He breaks the kiss with a groan, as frantic as me as I grab the bottom of my velvet, black shirt and slip it over my head.

Needing him, I work his belt open as he grabs the back of his shirt with his fist and pulls it over his head. My knuckles graze his abs as I open the button of his jeans, mouth practically watering as I shove them down his muscular thighs. His cock is hard, thick, and bouncing above his belly button with the metal piercing holding all my attention. Tey grasps my thong, pulling it down my thighs and legs as I shift up onto my knees to drag my panties off. I fling them in the front seat and grab his cock as I position myself over him, my pussy soaking wet.

"Wait," he says, making me freeze as he scrunches his eyebrows and pulls his unicorn out of his pocket.

I smile, watching in fascination as he lifts the tail and pulls out the world's smallest bottle of lube. He flips the cap and squirts it on the tip of his cock, sliding his hand up and down until he's completely coated. He looks at me and chuckles under his breath at my arched brow.

"Peaches, you're wet and bloody but I'm still big. I want you to enjoy this too." He carefully sets his stuffed animal in the seat next to us and places his big hands on my waist.

I squeeze his hard cock again, rubbing him back and forth over my clit as my hips roll before positioning him at my entrance. I gasp, the thick tip of his cock sliding inside when I start to lower my body onto his. I should feel embarrassed at hearing how wet I am but all I can focus on is his piercing grazing the inner walls of my pussy the more I sink onto him.

"Damn, Tillie, that's a beautiful sight," he breathes out, his gaze focused between us as he watches me glide his cock halfway in and out.

I glance down, clasping my hands behind his neck for something to hold onto as my belly tightens in pleasure. I shift, grinding on him and seeing my juices mixed together with my blood on his cock just before I take a deep breath and slam the rest of the way down on him with a scream leaving my mouth. He hisses, sliding farther down on the leather seats as his hands hold my waist so tight I know I'm going to have bruises.

"Tey." I whimper, setting my forehead against his as I play with his light blond hair on his neck.

"I know, sweets. You feel fucking amazing and incredible when you squeeze my cock just like that." He groans, slamming his head against the headrest as my pussy flexes around his length to tease him.

He flicks the clasp of my bra open and slides it down my arms, throwing it in the front seat with my panties. I lean against him, crossing my wrist behind his head as my breasts touch the hard planes of his chest. My nipples are extra sensitive from my period, I can't stop moaning and grinding against him as I tease my hard nipples along his pecs. My clit rubs against his tight abs as my hips roll, I squeeze my eyes shut on how good it feels.

"Open your eyes and look at the mess you're making," he demands, sliding me halfway off him with his biceps flexing as I open my eyes and lean away from him to glance down.

His cock is glistening with my blood and cream dripping down his length. I bite my bottom lip as I see his thighs covered with my blood, making it look like angel wings on either side.

"So fucking dirty. Keep making a mess, angel, let's piss off Nicky." His lips spread into a crazed smile and he slams me back down on him before gliding me back up by the waist.

My scream is loud even to my own ears, I kiss him as I start to match the rhythm he started. Sliding up and down his cock, I place my forehead on his shoulder as pleasure makes my eyes roll to the back of my head. I know anyone outside will see the car bouncing roughly, each time our bodies slap together the car moves and fills with sounds and our moans. He grabs my hair and pulls, making my back arch as he drags me away from him. He bends his head, biting my nipple until it stings, and sucks it into his hot mouth, hard. His mouth switches back and forth between my breasts, leaving bruises all over. My nipples throb painfully, his teeth bite lightly into my flesh and tugs until I'm rocking against him so hard to chase after the ecstasy pulsing through my veins.

"Tey, I–I need—" I can't even get the words out, my body

is riding on bliss and the toxicness of him that I can't get enough of.

"I know what you need," he says in a dark, wicked voice that sends a shiver down my spine.

He slides one hand down to my ass, squeezes as his other hand grabs my wrist and places my fingers on his choker. I slide off him and sink back down on him faster and faster without breaking my gaze away from his as I twist the choker around his neck. I keep a tight hold, watching his neck muscles strain, his veins pulsing as he leans his head back with a pleased sigh. I cut off his air, riding him like my life depends on it. When his face starts to turn a deep shade of red, I release the choker and place both of my hands on the ceiling to balance myself and pick up my pace even more. The car rocks hard with each movement, and he trails his other hand down my spine until he grasps both of my ass cheeks in his calloused palms. He helps guide my body, holding me still as he drives up inside me from below. My throat becomes hoarse as a scream of pleasure leaves my lips, my whole body trembling with sweat sliding down my back.

"I'm going to fill you up with my cum. So much cum. Be a good girl and take it all." He groans, his pupils blown wide and I can feel his cock twitching inside of me as he slides in and out roughly, my breasts bouncing in his face.

"You're."

Thrust.

"My good."

Thrust.

"Fucking girl."

Thrust. Thrust.

My orgasm rushes through me as he thrusts hard into me, my eyes rolling into the back of my head. I lean back to leave some space between us as he squeezes my hips quickly to pull me off of him so he can watch me squirt all over his cock and lower abs. He slams back inside of me forcefully with a harsh groan, holding my shaking thighs as I feel him start to come. Ropes and ropes of his thick cum coats the inside of my pussy, making a wet, crude noise as he fucks me frantically through his orgasm. He can't seem to stop coming as he holds himself still inside of me, letting me feel every twitch of his cock. His sticky cum is leaking out of me and sliding down my thighs to mix with my cum and blood. I can't stop grinding my clit on him to prolong my orgasm, feeling his piercing rubbing my inner walls deliciously.

"That was… amazing." I gasp, trying to catch my breath as my body gives small shivers.

"Thanks for making my dreams a reality," he says dreamily, pulling me close as his chest heaves up and down.

My arms collapse from the roof of the car and onto the headrest behind Tey. I feel heavy and like I could sleep for a year straight as my body relaxes against his.

"Anytime. Seriously, anytime." His dark chuckle sounds in my ear as I sigh into his neck.

"I'll hold you to that." He slides his fingers through my hair, almost making me purr at how good it feels.

I draw in a deep breath and slip away from him, staring at his blue eyes that see into my soul.

"My love for you goes deeper than just my heart, Tey. We were always meant to find each other. My broken soul and your twisted one. Thank you for bringing me to life."

CHAPTER 16

Tey

My breath catches in the back of my throat. That's all I wanted to do for her. Take her soul and keep it safe so she can live. Make her a little bloody in the process. My dark, sinister side will always be inside of me and she accepts that without any questions.

She's perfect. Everything we ever needed.

"Always," I mutter quietly, dropping my head back against the headrest as my thoughts race that she loves me.

The twisted, crazy, scary, blue-eyed fucker that I am.

"Nicky is going to kill us," she whispers with a smile in her voice and I look at her to see her gaze directed down to the sticky mess of cum and blood on the seats.

Following her gaze, my lips spread into a pleased as fuck grin at all the blood and cum. I might get addicted to this sight. Her sitting on my lap, blood coating my cock and thighs. Her face is smeared with more blood from the cut on her lip, making me feel like a sick animal inside at being obsessed but you can't change a person when they've been this way their whole life. Bright red and flowing with the pounding of her heart, her blood holds all my attention. All mine.

"Maybe but I'm not done with you yet. Crawl in the front

seat for me, love." You can't hide the devilish excitement in my voice.

"I'm suddenly scared." She arches an eyebrow, flicking her gaze up and down at me in suspicion.

She shakes her head and starts to slip off my lap, hissing between her teeth when she sits her ass on the console between the front seats. I'm not a small man by any means and if you've never taken a pierced cock before, it can ache the first time. The view in front of me could tempt a priest to commit a sin. With her legs spread wide, she grimaces as she glances down at her puffy, sore pussy. She starts to close her legs but I place my palms on her inner thighs to stop her.

"Have to make sure you feel me for days." I glide two fingers through the sticky, lovely mess leaking out of her wrecked pussy and shove our cum back inside her.

She grabs the seats on either side of her with a sharp hiss leaving her parted lips and watches as I pump my fingers in and out. I hold my fingers still inside her, crooking them against a spot that makes her back arch and has her cursing under her breath. She starts to shift her hips, trying to make me move my fingers but I pull them out and see all my thick, light pink cum seeping out of her slowly.

"I hate you right now. Why does it always feel good even when you guys cause me pain?" She breathes out a drawn out exhale and twists to crawl in the front passenger seat to slip on her bra.

"You love it when we hurt you. It excites you and pisses you off at the same time." My voice comes out husky, imagining all the pain I can cause her.

She hooks her bra on as I pull my pants up my thighs, leaving the button undone and sitting here shirtless as I gaze at her grumbling under her breath. I grab my phone out of my jeans pocket, going to my camera and pointing it right at her. She grabs her shirt off the floorboard and is just about to slip it over her head when I stop her.

"Why don't you show the guys how much of a good girl you are." She glances over her shoulder at me, maybe hearing the sudden deepening of my voice filled with lust.

She glances at my phone and drops her shirt without hesitation.

"Where do you want me?" She bites her bottom lip teasingly, her voice raspy as she stares at the camera.

"Face towards the windshield," I command wickedly, feeling my dick jerk in my pants as she listens without hesitating and faces away from me with her beautiful ass swaying side to side, driving me crazy. I want to bite her tempting ass.

"Now what?" Her voice is sexy and seductive.

"I think you should take the stick shift for a test drive, don't you?" I glance away from the screen of my camera as she freezes, seeing her shoulder move with a deep inhale.

After a second, she moves, shifting her knees over on either side of the front seats until she's hovering over the stick shift. Her ass is a beautiful sight, thick and juicy as her skirt pools around her waist. She reaches for her underwear on the passenger seat and uses it to gather her hair into a high ponytail so her whole back is exposed for the camera. Shit. I'll be stealing those panties later to keep. She places her hands on the dashboard as she lowers over the stick shift. My gaze trails down her arched back, taking in her tattoos and scars, all the way down to her smooth, bubbly ass.

"How's it feel, baby girl?" I ask, using Logan's nickname and knowing it's going to piss him off when he receives the video.

"Strange but good. Nicky won't be able to go anywhere without thinking of me, smelling both of us in his car." She moans, leaning farther forward as she slides up slowly on the stick shift.

Her pussy is red and swollen from taking my cock but it still grips the stick shift and leaves behind evidence of our fucking. The guys are going to lose it, I feel like I'm about to lose my mind seeing my cum dripping all over the place. I turn off the camera just as she sinks back down with a loud moan and send the video in the group chat real quick before tossing my phone on the seat. I'm really glad the guys, minus Dalton, are in class, jealous fuckers are going to go crazy once they get the video of our girl.

"Get back here. I'm ready for round two." Never have I sounded so needy, my cock desperate for her again.

"Oh God." She groans, easing off the stick shift, and turns around with heated eyes as she moves as fast as she can between the seats.

She's as desperate as me. This woman is meant to be mine, I'll kill anyone who tries to take her away.

My phone starts to go crazy, buzzing with incoming texts and ringing when I ignore them. I'm busy, about to fuck our girl. They can fucking wait. She eases into the seat next to me, bending back as I follow her down and brace myself on my forearms on either side of her.

"Tey," she begs, wrapping her wrists behind my head to drag me closer and crossing her ankles behind my lower back to hold me hostage.

I'm not going anywhere.

The backseat car door suddenly opening has my head whipping up, my eyes going wide at the gun pointed at my head. My lips twist into a snarl, seeing the masked asshole daring to look at my woman, her mostly naked body on display.

"You're a dead man," I growl out, starting to sit up as Tillie gasps when she arches her head back to see a stranger with a gun in the open door.

The man whips the butt of his gun across my face,

making my head snap to the side and cutting open the skin on the corner of my eye. I can hear Tillie screaming as all the doors open. Someone grabs me from behind as Tillie is dragged out of the car kicking and cursing. I'm thrown to the pavement of the parking lot, booted feet immediately kicking at me from all angles before I can slaughter them. The breath rushes out of me from the blow to the kidneys, making bile crawl up my throat.

"Don't kill him! He comes with us!" One of the men shouts out orders, his face hidden behind a black mask but I spot the gang symbol of a cobra snake tattoo peeking out from the sleeve of his shirt.

Fucking Los Muerte gang.

They haul me to my feet, dragging me around the back of Nicky's car towards a blue Cadillac with the trunk open. I struggle in their grip, fighting harder as I see one of them trying to shove Tillie into the back of the trunk.

"I'm going to kill you all! I'll start with your toes and make my way up, keeping you alive long enough as I peel layer after layer of your skin!" I say in a deadly voice, feeling their gazes on me as each one of them freeze in place.

I can practically smell their fear, they know who the fuck I am. I don't make threats and not follow through.

My gaze connects with Tillie's eyes, seeing her strength as she doesn't stop fighting. I roar with my rage when the man trying to shove her in the trunk grabs her breast over her bra with a chuckle. He's the first to go... I think Tillie has the same thought, she quickly reaches for the knife strapped to the man's thigh without hesitating. My smile is feral, the copper taste filling my mouth as blood drips down my face but I've never been more proud of her as I am right now.

She slashes her hand across his throat with the knife, his eyes widening as a river of blood flows from the cut from one side of his neck to the other and soaks her face in a spray of blood. The guy drops like a bag of stones, dead. Tillie starts to run towards me with the knife raised over her head with a scream like she's going to save me but one of the masked guys sneaks up behind her. He grabs her hair roughly and swings her around, knocking her head against the edge of the bumper. She falls to the ground, grabbing her bleeding head as she sits up.

"You killed Ethan! You fucking bitch!" one of the masked fuckers yells in Tillie's face before he hauls up by her elbow and throws her in the trunk.

I try to break free, fighting with everything inside of me as the two men holding my arms drag me kicking and struggling over to the trunk. I'm tossed in beside Tillie within seconds and zip tied by my ankles along with my wrists.

"You deserve what's coming to you, cunt. Cruz is very, very excited to see you." one of the masked men snarls in our faces and slams the trunk closed, shutting us in the dark.

"No. No. No," Tillie chants, her breath fanning across my face.

Cruz.

The fucking psychopath that hurt my woman time and time again.

I can't wait to meet him.

I'm going to string him upside down, cut his throat open, and wait until all his blood drains out of his body before leaving him in the desert for the coyotes to chew on.

"Shhh. It's going to be okay, Tillie. I'm right here and not going anywhere without you." I scoot closer to her, wiggling until the front of my body presses against her soft one.

"Tey," she rasps, sounding fucking terrified.

"Don't worry, he'll pay, sweetheart. You'll get your revenge," I mutter into her hair, my breath coming in big pants as the promise leaves my lips.

I'll make sure vengeance is hers.

EPILOGUE

Cruz

*F**inally**.*

The end for now...

AUTHOR'S NOTE

Sooooo... How are we doing?! Everyone okay? Take a deep breath and don't throw your kindle or come at me with a deep hatred for that cliffy. I can't wait to hear about your reactions to this book and theories that will all be uncovered in part four. I love all my readers and hope you enjoyed this book even though I'm leaving you guys hanging until the next book. The final freaking book in this series. It's been a wild ride. Thank you so much for reading, sharing, and reviewing.

STALKING LINKS FOR MADELINE FAY

Facebook Group:
https://www.facebook.com/groups/270252770540820/

Newsletter: https://www.subscribepage.com/MadelineFayNL

Facebook like page:
https://www.facebook.com/madelinefayauthor/

Instagram: http://Instagram.com/Madelinefay_author/

TikTok: www.tiktok.com/@madelinefayauthor

ABOUT MADELINE FAY

Madeline lives in rural Michigan in a castle with all her fur babies and husband. She loves to read, you'll find her in her tower with her kindle and drinking Boba tea. She has a few addictions, chocolate is her weakness and anything seventies related. She's a hippy at heart. She likes to pretend she's a main character in a Korean drama and listens to Kpop, mainly BTS. She has an evil day job, but at night she watches over her city in the shadows and calls herself Batman. Not really but she keeps hoping it might come true one day. She's in her bat cave writing and plotting mad, evil genius stories while sipping some wine.

9 798886 917125 2